Quest of the Snow Leopard

Also by Roy Chapman Andrews

QUEST IN THE DESERT

Quest of the Snow Leopard

BY ROY CHAPMAN ANDREWS

Illustrated by Kurt Wiese

THE VIKING PRESS · NEW YORK

PRINTED IN THE U.S.A. BY THE VAIL-BALLOU PRESS, INC.

This book is dedicated

to

Boy Scouts everywhere

Contents

Quest of the Snow Leopard

1. Ken's Man-Eater

KEN LEWIS couldn't believe it was true! Only a month ago he had walked the streets of New York; today he was sitting in a tent on the outskirts of a village in South China, waiting to shoot a man-eating tiger! But it *was* true. Jack Benton sat there too, cleaning his rifle and placing big cartridges in a neat row on the camp table. Ken could hear the strange babel of Chinese talk from the village, and sniff unfamiliar smells. Through the tent door, terraced rice paddies showed like giant green stairs, climbing up the valley between hills clothed with swordgrass. It was China, just as he had imagined it.

From his brown leather wallet he took out the letter of appointment from the Natural History Museum. He had read it a dozen times, at least, during the trip across the Pacific and down the China coast from Shanghai to Foochow. He knew every line by heart, but it still was exciting actually to see the words and the gold seal with the two short blue ribbons. The letter was dated June 12, 1916, and it read,

Dear Mr. Lewis:

It gives me much pleasure to confirm our conversation and hand you this letter of appointment to the Chinese Zoological Expedition under the leadership of Mr. John Benton. The terms of the engagement are as follows:

1. The period will be for the duration of the expedition, approximately one year.

2. All your expenses will be paid from the time you leave New York until your return. In addition you will receive a salary of fifty dollars per month.

3. You are to join Mr. Benton in China, wherever he directs, by the first ship.

4. The object of the expedition is to explore the mountains of southwest China and eastern Tibet for the purpose of zoological collecting.

5. A particular desideratum is to obtain specimens of the Tibetan snow leopard, which, to the best of our knowledge, has never been killed or captured by a white man.

6. Since the region you are to explore is known to be inhabited by natives who may be unfriendly, some personal danger may be involved. You are cognizant of this fact, and are joining the expedition with the full consent of your parents. Therefore, this letter will be considered to release the Museum from any indemnity claim in the event of your serious injury or death. Both copies should be signed by your mother and father, since you are a minor, as well as by yourself.

I wish to express our appreciation of the excellent volunteer work you have done in the Museum during the past two years, and congratulate you upon this opportunity to engage in field work under the direction of one of our most experienced and able explorers.

Faithfully yours,
James Fennimore
Director

Accepted: Kenneth Lewis
Arthur T. Lewis
Carolyn A. Lewis

Ken folded the letter and replaced it in his wallet. He was a tall boy, almost six feet, with what would be a powerful body when the years put more flesh on his bones. Clear gray eyes gazed out from a sun-tanned face. His mouth still had the softness of youth, but the chin was firm and strong.

Benton looked up with a smile. "Hard to believe, isn't it?" he said. "I know how you feel; I was the same way when I went on my first expedition. Let's see, you will be seventeen in two weeks. You've beaten me by a little more than a month. I left New York for my first trip on my seventeenth birthday. It's strange how your life has been almost a parallel to mine so far. Both of us always intended to be naturalists and explorers ever since we could remember. We knew we couldn't be happy doing anything else. We were both Eagle Scouts; we both worked in the zoo and the museum as volunteer assistants. That's how I first met Alex Chapin and went to Manchuria with him, and how you and I became friends. Now you're in China with me. It *is* strange. We're two birds out of the same nest, even though I hatched earlier than you did. I'm twenty-seven, and already I've spent the best part of ten years in Asia. I'll get a great kick out of passing on to you what I have learned about the Orient, just as Alex passed it on to me. After he was killed by bandits I was ready to carry on the job that he had started."

"It's wonderful," Ken said. "When I met you, and you let me work with you on your Chinese collections, I was happier than I've ever been in my life. Now we're here together in China, and I'll see the same animals alive that I handled in the museum. I never thought that dream could come true."

"Most dreams come true, Ken, if you work hard enough to make them. They don't just happen without any effort. I don't believe much in what people call 'luck.' You make your own luck by hard work and enthusiasm. If you hadn't done such a good job on my collections, I'd never have asked you to come on this trip. It's going to be tough, and I wanted someone who would love the job enough to take the thick with the thin. There'll be plenty of excitement before we get back, for that whole country of Yunnan and the Tibetan frontier is pretty disturbed, and many of the aboriginal tribesmen have never seen a white man. We will be just like the pioneers in the Indian-fighting days of our Old West—on the watch for trouble every minute. As I told you this morning when I met you at the ship, I don't want to go there until August, because the rains won't end before early September. That's the reason I stopped off here when I heard about this black tiger."

"Do you think it is a new species?"

"No, I don't. I believe it is a melanistic phase of the ordinary yellow tiger. You know, melanism is an excess of *melanin*, the coloring matter in the skin; it's the opposite of albinism, where there is no coloring matter at all. Melanism is very common in some animals, such as squirrels, rabbits, foxes, and leopards, but it is rare in others; a black tiger never has been reported. If we could get him it would be a ten strike."

"What does he look like?"

"A missionary I know has seen him two or three times at close range. He says the ground color of the body is dark maltese, changing into beautiful light blue on the lower sides and belly. The stripes are black and well defined, like those on a yellow tiger. The natives in this village describe the tiger the same way. He is a man-eater, and a pretty nasty customer, I guess. Already this year he has killed sixteen people, and the villagers are terrified. They think he is some kind of evil spirit. Only last week he took a child in that house over there on the edge of the rice fields. The family was eating dinner while the baby played in the courtyard. Suddenly the black tiger rushed through the door and grabbed the child. He stood for a moment and then leaped over the wall with the baby in his mouth. A dozen men, beating pans, followed him up the valley, but they found only a little shoe and a bloody rag on a thorn bush."

"Do you think I'll get a chance to kill a tiger, Jack?"

"You certainly will. This region swarms with them. I'll be surprised if we don't get two or three in the next few weeks; but this black devil is very special, and I'll have to shoot first. I hope you don't mind. I know what a wonderful shot you are, but you haven't had the experience and you don't know what a terrifying thing it is to see a wild tiger glaring at you only a few feet away. It's not like riding on the back of an elephant, or sitting on a *machan* up in a tree—the way they hunt tigers in India. In this kind of hunting, if you don't kill him, the tiger will probably kill you. The first one I shot was only ten feet from me, and I was shaking so I could hardly hold the rifle. How I ever hit him I'll never know. Just luck, I guess."

"Of course I understand. I'll probably be scared stiff. I've looked at tigers in the zoo and wondered how I'd feel if there weren't any bars between us. It used to make me shiver."

By three o'clock that afternoon the men were on their way through the rice paddies, dragging two reluctant goats, a mother and her nursing kid. At the entrance to a narrow ravine Benton halted.

"This is where the black tiger lives, and I'll bet he's home. We'll tie the goats in this little open space and get behind those bushes."

"Great Scott, Jack, he'll be almost in our laps when he comes out!"

"Can't be helped; there isn't any other spot. I know this lair like the palm of my hand. I killed my first tiger right on that terrace."

It was a devilish place, a deep cut in the mountain, choked with thorny vines and swordgrass. Three or four dark tunnels twisted, snakelike, back into the murderous growth. "Tiger paths," Benton said laconically. "I crawled up that one on the right for about twenty feet one day. Found a sort of room with bones of all kinds, a human skull, and heaps of pangolin scales— tigers love pangolins. Branch tunnels went off in three directions. Then I realized what a foolish thing I'd done. My scalp began to prickle, and I backed out in a hurry."

For three hours they sat motionless, watching the shadows steal down the ravine and reach a lone palm tree on the bare opposite ridge. Ken's watch indicated half-past six; that meant another hour of waiting, not more, for darkness comes swiftly in the South China hills. Suddenly the mother goat gave a terrified blat and tugged frantically at her rope, staring across the ravine. Right in the open, beside the palm tree, crouched a long yellow and black body. Ken rubbed his eyes. It hadn't been there a moment before; it had taken shape and substance out of nothing, like a ghost. He glanced at Benton. Jack put his mouth close to Ken's ear and whispered, "It's a tigress. She doesn't belong in this lair. She came from over the ridge—heard the goats. We can't shoot her where she is—too far. She'll come here, I think. We've got to wait. You may shoot first. Hold low. Understand?"

Ken nodded. The tigress seemed to suspect danger, seeing the goats in that unusual place with no Chinese near them. She crouched beside the palm tree like an enormous tabby cat, sometimes stretching one foot forward as though about to move, but each time drawing it back again. Ken was half kneeling, his rifle pushed forward. A drop of sweat trickled down his nose, divided, and ran into the corners of his mouth. He could taste the salt of the sweat. Another drop started above his left eye, and he blinked frantically. Benton sat like a stone Buddha, the stock of his rifle nestled under his armpit. Twenty minutes dragged by; they seemed twenty hours. A "brain-fever bird" on a tree above them kept giving the rising, breathless call that drives people crazy in the jungle heat. Lord! Ken thought. Why doesn't something happen? I can't stand this much longer!

At last the tigress rose and circled to reach a tiny path. She had to cross a small bare space—it was only about twenty feet —but apparently she didn't like being in the open. She flattened like a snake, her chin and throat touching the ground, and slithered along with no body motion that they could see except the quivering of her shoulders and hips. Yet she went very fast. Once in cover again, she made three flying leaps toward the goats. The last one brought her face to face with the men not fifteen feet away. Utterly surprised, she stood there snarling, her green eyes blazing, ears laid back.

Ken had been shaking violently, but in the instant for action his nerves tightened like threads of steel. Holding his aim low on her breast, he squeezed the trigger. The heavy rifle slammed hard against his shoulder. The tigress threw up her head and reared back, sliding slowly down the terrace. On the instant, Benton's shot roared in Ken's ear. The great beast stretched out, quivered, and lay still.

Ken sank down beside Jack. He was trembling, and his knees felt weak. "Did I hit her?" He gasped.

"I'll say you did! I only fired to make sure. You've killed your first tiger. Did it like a veteran. I'm proud of you, boy. By gosh, I *am* proud of you!"

After five minutes, during which the tigress did not move, with rifles ready, they slipped down the terrace to the great yellow and black body. The animal was stone dead.

Benton lifted one forepaw. "Ken, you got her right in the chest. I'll bet when we skin her we'll find the heart is smashed to pulp. She'd have been on our necks if you had missed."

Ken had never been so happy. He would remember that moment and Benton's words all his life.

"What will we do now, Jack? Skin her here?"

"No, sit down and smoke a pipe. It won't be long. The people in the village will have heard the shots. We'll have a dozen men here before half an hour to carry her back. Then you'll have a surprise."

"What do you mean, 'surprise'?"

"You'll see. They put on quite a show when a dead tiger is in their hands."

In less than twenty minutes shouts sounded down the trail. Benton answered, and a line of men burst through the sword-grass, carrying ropes and a long pole. For a moment the group stood silent, gazing at the dead animal. "But it isn't the black tiger, *Shen-shung*. We thought surely you had killed the black tiger."

"No, we didn't see him. This one got here first. She came

from over the ridge. Maybe we will get the black tiger tomorrow."

When they reached the village the mother of the baby the black tiger had killed began beating the dead animal with a stick, screaming curses on all the tiger tribe.

"Watch them carefully, Ken," Benton said. "When they skin her they'll try to cut off the whiskers and claws. Those make the best medicine. I've told the head man they can have the body, but we want the hide, skull, and legbones."

As the Chinese stripped off the skin, every drop of blood was sopped up with rags. These the villagers tied about their necks to ward off disease and personal devils.

"They'll sell the flesh," Jack said. "Anyone who eats a small piece is supposed to acquire some of the tiger's courage. All the bones will be stewed up into a kind of jelly. After it cools and hardens they mold it into pills and sell them to Chinese druggists in Futsing. The village will make about four hundred dollars out of the carcass."

"Jack, do you think it was a man-eating tigress? I'd like to be able to say I'd killed a man-eater."

"You can say that, all right. Virtually all these South China tigers are man-eaters. In India they think most habitual man-eaters are old beasts that find it hard to kill game in the jungle; also, that when they have had a taste of human flesh they like it better than any other meat. I don't believe that part is true. It certainly isn't of the tigers in this region. Game is not very plentiful here, and so the tigers live near the villages. They take pigs, goats, cows and dogs, and, now and then, a person—children, mostly. I guess that's because boys are often with the cattle, or are gathering wood on the hills. But sometimes they come right into the courtyards and grab a child—as that one did last week. They are extraordinary beasts, a mixture of daring courage and great cowardice. The one thing they seem to be terrified of is the human voice. I know of a dozen cases where a tiger has dropped its kill when someone yelled."

"But the black tiger didn't, and I'll bet everyone was screaming at the top of his voice."

"That's true, but you can't generalize. Sometimes one won't follow the usual pattern, but if you ever get in a tight fix with a tiger, yell like a banshee. Right near this village a man was walking back from the rice paddies when a tiger jumped out from behind a bush and grabbed him by the arm. The poor fellow hung on to a branch and began to scream. The tiger dropped him like a hot potato and ducked back into the jungle.

"They like the mangy Chinese dogs better than a fat goat or a cow—frogs, too. Often they'll spend a whole night hunting frogs on the dikes by the rice paddies. Once, when I was shooting about twenty miles from here, I sent my boy out to get some frogs. I like to eat their legs, and these are real busters— almost as big as chicken legs. The boy had half a dozen frogs tied up in a cloth. They were all alive and croaking like mad. He started back to camp along a trail bordered with sword-grass. Suddenly a tiger jumped out, swung his paw, knocking the bag out of the boy's hand, and dashed off up the trail."

"What are we going to do about the black tiger, Jack? Do you suppose he is still in the big ravine?"

"I don't know. Every one of these tigers seems to have its own particular beat, moving from village to village in a circle and never spending more than a day or two in any one lair. We'll go up tomorrow and have another try. Maybe he'll be there; maybe not. If he isn't, we'll sit tight here and wait until someone brings us word. The natives will do that quickly enough if he turns up in another place. They'd give just about anything to have us kill that beast."

II. The Black Tiger

THE next afternoon Jack and Ken again took the two goats into the big ravine. Nothing happened. For nearly four hours they sat in the broiling sun, motionless. The brain-fever bird was still there, and once a muntjac, the tiny barking deer of South China, ventured out to investigate the goats.

"Gosh, I'd like to shoot that little fellow," Jack whispered. "They're the best eating of all the game in China. But we'd spoil our chance at the tiger if we did. When you get your teeth into a muntjac fillet you'll know what I mean."

The following day was a repetition of the other, except for

the muntjac. The brain-fever bird and the two men had the shimmering, heat-filled lair to themselves. On the third morning a breathless Chinese arrived in camp from a village four miles away.

"The black tiger came right into the street," he reported, panting, "and grabbed a dog. He threw it over his shoulder like a sack of rice and ran off to the hills. Everyone followed, yelling and beating pans, and just inside the grass, on an old terrace, he dropped the dog. It's there; we found it."

Benton was electrified. "This time we'll get him alive, Ken. If a tiger hasn't finished his kill, he'll always come back after dark. We'll set a trap. I'll bet a dollar to a plugged nickel we'll have him in the morning."

They hurried to the village. Dozens of excited men wanted to show them the dog, but Benton selected only two and told the others to make a cage of heavy bamboo poles.

"We'll catch the black tiger for you tonight," he said. "I speak the truth." They looked dubious but examined the huge steel trap with interest. Ken clamped the vises on the springs, screwed them down, and set the trap. Then Wang, the Elder of the village, touched the pan with a heavy stick, and the jaws snapped shut. Three boys tried to pull it out; it wouldn't budge.

"That," the Elder pronounced, "is a good trap. Never has its like been seen in China. It will hold the black tiger or any other tiger—but," he added slyly, "first he must get in it. I doubt that he ever will."

They found the dog lying beside a tree on a terrace about five feet wide, just above the open rice fields. Its skull was crushed, probably from the first blow of the tiger's paw, but only teethmarks showed on the body. "It couldn't be better,"

Jack said. They buried the trap on the terrace and fastened the dog to the tree with heavy wire.

"He's bound to come from above and probably will eat the dog right here. It isn't possible he won't be caught."

Benton and Ken slept that night in the village. After sunrise at least fifty men, women, and boys accompanied them to the trap, bearing a cage strong enough to hold a gorilla. Benton halted the crowd a hundred yards away and, with Ken, approached the terrace, rifle ready.

Silence!

"I wonder what's wrong, Ken? He ought to be raising Cain."

Foot by foot they crept forward, but not a sound broke the stillness of the jungle. At last they could see the trap. There was no tiger, and the dog was gone! They stared in amazement.

"It just can't be," Jack said. But it was! The story showed all too plainly. The black tiger had approached from above, as they had expected, had dropped his forefeet on the terrace, reached over, and lifted the dog from the tree as though it had been tied with thread. Then he had eaten it comfortably on the upper dike a few feet away. The claw marks were within an inch of the trap pan. Just one inch more, and they'd have had him! The villagers crowded about like a jury to examine the evidence. Collectively they shook their heads, and old Wang delivered the verdict.

"Some years ago Sheng, as you well know, killed his father. He was given the Death of a Thousand Cuts, but nothing was done by our village to atone for his crime. The gods were offended. Now they have sent this black tiger to harass our dwelling place. It is not a 'proper' tiger. No one can trap or kill an evil spirit!"

Two days later, news of the black tiger came again. It had

jumped into a cowpen beside a house, killed a yearling heifer, and leaped out with the dead animal in its mouth. Benton measured the fence; it was twelve feet high. Such a performance seemed almost impossible, but the farmer and his wife were eyewitnesses. Natives discovered the remains of the calf, only half eaten, about two miles away. Benton and Ken were on the spot early in the afternoon. The carcass was in a bad place—a very bad place. Four or five animal trails led to a tiny open space with a pool of water, in the midst of very thick jungle. The only way they could see the heifer was by sitting in one of the paths, for they did not dare touch the body.

Benton looked about uneasily. "I don't like this at all. A tiger always moves along a trail if he can, and he might come down this one."

"But Jack, with all these other paths, why should he come this way?"

"I still don't like it. We're taking a big chance, and you need make only one mistake with a tiger. But there's no other spot. We'll have to risk it, I guess."

The men settled themselves in the tall swordgrass, rifles ready. They had been watching for an hour when Jack thought he heard the low rumble of thunder. Ken heard it too, and both looked up; there wasn't a cloud in the sunlit sky. Then the rumble came again, this time ending in a snarl. A tiger was right behind them in the grass! Benton knew the animal was near enough to spring, else it wouldn't have growled. He couldn't see the beast, but he was sure any sudden move would bring it on them. There was just one chance—take it by surprise. He twisted around very, very slowly, and the tiger snarled again. Probably it didn't attack because it was completely taken aback to find the men on the trail. Suddenly Benton yelled and leaped forward, but caught his foot in a vine and sprawled on his face, arms outstretched. *His left hand actually slapped the tiger on the nose!* The beast went right over backward, whirled, and in one jump disappeared in the grass.

Benton couldn't have fired, even if he hadn't dropped his rifle. He and Ken stood shaking for a time, sweat pouring off their faces; then both got awfully sick. Violent nausea doubled them up in spasms of retching and coughing.

"I want to get out of here," Ken quavered.

Jack waved his hand. "I do too. Let's go."

Back in camp, they gulped cups of strong tea.

"That," said Benton, "was the closest to a most unpleasant death that I've ever come. I've learned my lesson, and I hope you have. It just doesn't pay to take chances with a tiger. They always do the unexpected."

A week later the black tiger killed again seven miles from their camp. He was asleep on a grass-covered terrace when a dozen fuel-gatherers disturbed him. The enraged beast leaped to his feet and dashed into the group, striking right and left with his great paws. One man's skull was crushed, another's head ripped half off his shoulders; a third landed ten feet away, with a broken neck, on a lower dike. Then the tiger jumped to an abandoned terrace, stood for a moment, growling, and turned into the grass. He made no attempt to drag off any of his victims; apparently the killing was out of sheer bad temper at being disturbed.

Word reached Benton at three o'clock. He and Ken almost ran the seven miles. "He's sure to return this afternoon," Jack said. "We've got to get there before he comes."

For two wretched hours they sat behind a bush near the terrace where the men had been killed. It was terribly hot! The thermometer had registered over 106 degrees in the shade when they left, and the humidity must have been 90 per cent. Just as night closed in, the vague outlines of the black tiger showed against a background of feathery bamboo at the head of the valley. Crouched on a rice dike in the open, he surveyed the spot where he had killed the men that morning.

Benton whispered, "In another fifteen minutes it will be too dark to shoot. I'm going to try him from here."

He slowly pushed up his rifle and sighted along the barrel, then shook his head. "No good. I can't see him through the sights. There's only one thing to do unless we lose him again. I'll go out in the open and walk straight toward him until I'm near enough to see clearly. You'd better stay here."

"Nothing doing, Jack. If you go, I go. With both of us we'll have a double chance. I'm not scared."

To his surprise he wasn't frightened. To test himself he sighted his rifle. It held steady as a rock. Jack nodded and smiled. The two men rose from the grass and walked out onto the floor of the valley side by side. The tiger saw them instantly. He got to his feet and stood switching his tail, ears laid back, growling a deadly threat. At any moment they expected him to charge, but he seemed undecided, fascinated by their steady advance. Forty yards, thirty, twenty! The form of the great beast emerged in the dim light, clear and distinct; they could even see the black stripes on the dark body. The animal flattened and gathered itself for a spring, but waited a fraction of a second too long. After dropping on one knee, Benton fired. The shaft of yellow flame tore apart the South China night like a jagged flash of lightning. The tiger lunged into the air, twisted, and rolled down the terrace in a whirling ball, clawing at his side. He was almost at their feet when Ken's rifle roared. The bullet smashed the neck. With one convulsive quiver the black tiger stretched out, paws extended, like a giant sleeping cat.

For a long moment the men looked down at the beautiful blue-black body. Then suddenly the tension of wire-tight nerves loosened. With wild yells they pounded each other on the back and dashed about the terrace gathering grass for a beacon fire, piling on fuel until the flames shot high into the air. In less than half an hour the ravine swarmed with excited Chinese. They lashed the four-hundred-pound body to a carrying pole and started down the trail, chanting a barbaric song— a song out of China's dim past to celebrate victory in war!

There was no sleep for anyone that night. The news spread like wildfire to neighboring villages, and Chinese poured in to see the dreaded black tiger and perhaps get a bit of its flesh or a few drops of blood. Jack and Ken had their hands full to protect the animal from the relatives of people it had killed. Screaming curses, these people set upon it with spears and clubs. In a few minutes the body would have been beaten to a pulp, and the specimen ruined. Not until the skin was off could the men relax. As the sun rose in a hot, red ball from behind the eastern hills they tied the tent flaps and lay down on their camp cots. The last picture in Ken's mind was of the black tiger rolling down the terrace almost to his feet, and his glimpse of the snarling, clawing body through the sights of his rifle as he pressed the trigger. He wouldn't have changed places with anyone on earth.

III. The Pirates of Bias Bay

JACK and Ken slept until noon. As soon as breakfast was over Benton unrolled the heavily salted tiger skin and spread it out to dry in the sun. People were still arriving from neighboring villages, and a close-packed throng surrounded the tent, gazing in awed silence at the hide and skull of the dreaded beast.

"There isn't much doubt that this is a melanistic phase of the ordinary tiger," Jack said after he had made a comparison with the tigress Ken had killed. "But it is the first ever recorded. I imagine others will turn up in this region eventually." *

"Now that we have him, what shall we do?" Ken asked.

"I think our best bet is to go to Foochow and catch the first boat for Hong Kong. We may have to wait there several days. I don't want to do any more collecting here, for I spent a whole winter in this region three years ago and gave it a pretty careful going over. I must have caught most of the mammals of the region. By the time we have outfitted in Hong Kong and reach Yünnanfu the rainy season will have ended and the roads be passable. We'll hire a caravan of ponies at Yünnanfu and have at least three weeks' traveling before we get into the big mountains in the north. That's where we'll do our real work and hit unexplored country. Somewhere up there we'll find the snow leopard, I hope."

Benton asked the village head man for coolies to take their equipment to the seacoast, and shortly after daylight next morning a mob of chattering humanity surrounded their camp. Jack selected twenty of the strongest-looking men and turned them loose upon the pile of baggage. The coolies swarmed over it like flies, each one yelling at the top of his voice, tugging madly at the boxes and small fiber trunks. Ken was worried; it seemed that at any moment a battle to the death would engulf the camp.

"Can't you do something, Jack? They'll kill each other."

Benton laughed. "Don't worry. You'll learn that it is psychologically impossible for Chinese coolies to do anything quietly. They aren't a bit angry. Each one is trying to get the heaviest pieces, for they are paid according to weight. They can carry enormous loads on those poles. I've seen a man walk off happily with a hundred-and-twenty-five-pound trunk on each end of

* Others did. Three more were recorded in the next twenty years.

his staff. He'll carry it for six or eight miles and come in grinning."

True enough, the bedlam gradually quieted, and each coolie adjusted the ropes about his load, balancing one end against the other. Then they sat down in complete harmony to drink tea and smoke their diminutive pipes.

When the cavalcade finally started, half the village strung along the path between the rice fields, waving good-by to the men.

"We've made ourselves solid with these people," Benton said. "They'll never forget that we killed the black tiger. When you return, even if it is ten years from now, you'll have a warm welcome."

The raised path, barely wide enough for two people to pass abreast, wound like a snake among muddy rice fields on the floor of the wide valley. Every inch of ground was under cultivation. Even far up the hillsides, terraces rose tier upon tier. Villages almost overlapped, with only a few hundred yards between the last house of one and the first house of another. Human occupation to the point of saturation!

Ken gazed in amazement at the swarming blue-clad Chinese.

"I've often heard," he said, "about 'China's teeming millions.' Now I know what it means. But why are they all huddled up here? Why don't they spread out into the back country, where there is more room?"

"Because they are Chinese. That's the only answer. Chinese are gregarious by nature and hate to live alone. The closer they can get to their neighbors, the happier they are. Moreover, most of the people in these little villages are related by birth or marriage. Once their roots are sunk in the soil of one place, they will continue to live there generation after generation, no matter how crowded the country becomes. That's why they make every inch of land produce something, even if it is only a handful of garlic."

"Garlic is right. I can smell it everywhere."

"Wait till we reach Foochow. Then you'll really know what 'secondhand garlic' smells like."

"Is Yunnan, where we are going, anything like this?"

"Nothing—no more than Florida is like Alaska. You'll see forests and mountains such as you never dreamed of. We'll go for days without meeting a human being, and those we do see will be Tibetans or aboriginal tribesmen, not Chinese."

A little after noon they reached Foochow. Narrow stone-paved streets wandered in a seemingly aimless maze between open, evil-smelling sewers. Straw matting roofed the alleys, shutting out every ray of purifying sunlight. The air reeked with the stench of garlic, decay, and filth. The sweet, sickening odor of opium drifted out of many houses. Pigs, chickens, dogs, and ducks wandered in and out of shop doors, and children played, or slept, in the middle of the street.

Ken was horrified. "Good heavens, Jack, how can foreigners live in a place like this?"

"They don't. Their houses and offices are well out of the city, on that hill. You'll see in a few minutes, when we get to the Standard Oil Company's compound. The agent is a friend of mine, and we'll stay with him. Of course he doesn't know we are coming, but that won't make any difference."

Their cavalcade wound up the long slope to a big brick house in a walled compound. Bill Fanshaw, the agent, made them welcome with the casual hospitality of the East. The house was cool and charming. That evening they sat down at a table laid with white linen and gleaming silver. Soft-footed servants glided in and out of the dining room, bearing dishes of bamboo shoots, mushrooms, and half a dozen foods that were new to Ken. Above them the punkah, a short curtain pulled by a half-sleeping coolie, waved to and fro, keeping the heat-saturated air in constant motion. The life of a foreigner in China, Ken thought, is really not too difficult to take, after all!

"You won't have to wait for a boat," Bill Fanshaw said. "The *Sunkiang* is due in tonight. Harry Beecher is her captain. He's a grand chap—an Englishman. We'll have him up for tiffin—luncheon—tomorrow, and you can go aboard with him afterward, for I suppose he'll sail on the tide at sundown."

Captain Beecher did prove to be interesting. Even though he was only forty, he had been sailing the China coast between Tientsin and Hong Kong for twenty years. Into that time he had crammed more adventure and excitement than most men would have in two lifetimes. His tales of revolutions, bandits, and piracy sounded like a fiction thriller.

"It's a funny thing, this piracy," he said. "When I go back to England and tell how vessels are pirated on the China coast almost every week, no one will believe me. But it's true, all right."

Ken's eyes widened. "Do you mean pirates like Blackbeard and the ones that used to prowl about in the Caribbean?"

"Well, they aren't quite the same. These pirates don't sail with the Jolly Roger at the masthead and board a ship with knives between their teeth, or make people walk the plank, but that's only because the times and methods have changed. These fellows use automatics and machine guns and motor boats, and some of them dress like Chinese gentlemen. They're seagoing gangsters. They have a pirate hangout at Bias Bay, twenty-five miles north of Hong Kong, on the Chinese mainland. It's a region of craggy mountains with little fishing villages in deep, narrow bays. Pirates have used it for hundreds of years, and they'll go on using it for a hundred more."

"Why don't the British do something about it? Couldn't they destroy the place?"

"They could if they were free to do it, but they aren't. Hong Kong is only a tiny island, a British crown colony, near the Chinese mainland. The city is Victoria. The British can't send troops ashore to clean out the pirates at Bias Bay without trespassing on Chinese sovereignty and all that.

"A few years ago they did land Royal Marines at Bias Bay. They burned a few villages and half a dozen junks in retaliation for several British ships that had been snatched right from their front door, but it didn't do any good. The pirates simply disappeared into the hills. As soon as the Marines left they rebuilt their houses and continued as though nothing had happened. Moreover, it caused a lot of trouble with the Chinese."

"Why are all the pirates around Hong Kong, Captain? Don't they operate at other places?"

"No, they don't. You see, almost all the trade routes of the China coast and from the south focus there. Besides, it's a free port; there are no customs duties. Because it is so close to the Chinese mainland, where high tariffs are charged on all imports, it's the world's foremost center of smuggling. Some Chinese have become fabulously rich in that, and other kinds of illegal traffic, and they don't want anything done to spoil their business. They control the whole region on the mainland about Hong Kong. The officials are all in cahoots with them and get paid a big 'squeeze'—protection money, you'd call it in the States."

"How do the pirates go about it? Do they capture a ship and kill the crew, or let them go?" Ken asked.

"Sometimes they kill a few people, but that isn't often. The Hong Kong piracies are of two kinds—the big ones, which happen every year or two, where a gang masquerading as deck passengers goes aboard a vessel and, at a pre-arranged time, overpowers the officers and crew. The pirates may loot the ship and passengers and escape in a junk that comes alongside, or they may force the officers to sail the vessel up to Bias Bay. There they go through her at their leisure. If any rich Chinese are aboard, they hold them for ransom. The pirates have agents in various ports, and they know what the ship is carrying and if any wealthy travelers are on her.

"Big ones like that are the less frequent kind, but the little jobs happen almost every week. Pirate motor boats, armed with machine guns, overtake junks with valuable cargoes at night, stick up the crews, and make their getaway. It's really hijacking, for usually the junks are smugglers themselves."

To Benton and Fanshaw it was an old story, and, except when a big ship was pirated, they read the newspaper accounts with no more surprise than you would have at a mugging in New York's Central Park. But Ken Lewis hung on the captain's words with fascinated wonder. This was a China he had never dreamed existed. Piracy, he had supposed, had gone out of existence with the Spanish galleons and muzzle-loading cannon. That it flourished in the twentieth century, in his own day, seemed incredible. Even though treasure wasn't buried on lonely islands in leaden caskets, and the ships weren't scuttled by bearded ruffians with gold rings in their ears, the stories still held the inescapable romance and salty flavor of piracy on the high seas.

"Is there any chance of our being pirated on this trip?" he asked.

"Of course there's always a chance. The *Sunkiang* has been lucky. They only tried it once. That was three years ago, when I was mate. We had a mob of deck passengers that trip, and the pirates were among them, dressed as ordinary coolie Chinese. No one gives much attention to deck passengers. They pay their fare as they come aboard, and have to eat and sleep wherever they can find a place. They are allowed to wander about freely, so long as they don't go below. The pirates had bribed half a dozen members of the crew—they always do that—but one of them was the captain's boy. He got frightened and gave the show away. We were ready for them and captured the whole lot without firing a shot. We turned eleven pirates over to the authorities in Hong Kong, and a couple of weeks later they had a public hanging—wanted to make an example of them. It was a big show, but I didn't see it, for the *Sunkiang* was on her way back to Tientsin.

"We take all the precautions possible, but we'll probably get it one of these days. Of course you haven't seen it yet, but the bridge is surrounded by a steel grille, which is always kept locked. It's never opened except when the watch is changed every four hours. There's a light machine gun on the bridge, and all the officers wear revolvers when the ship is near Hong Kong. Still, the Chinese are clever and may try some new stunt. For the last six months we've had a full passenger list, and some of the passengers are wealthy Chinese. Plenty of valuable cargo, too. But the *Sunkiang* is no different from the other coastwise ships. They've all been doing a terrific business because of the war in the north. Still, I keep my fingers crossed on every trip."

The captain pushed back his chair. "Time for me to be getting down to the ship. I've a little paperwork to do before we sail. You chaps better come along within an hour. Ken will want to watch the deck passengers come aboard. It's a show for anyone who hasn't seen it."

Jack Benton and Ken got their things together. After saying

good-by to Bill Fanshaw, they followed a handcart with their baggage through the narrow streets of Foochow to the dock where the *Sunkiang* was tied up. Ken felt as though he were actually a part of China-coast history as he walked about the decks of the ship and looked up at the bridge, where Captain Beecher stood behind the steel grille. He could see the muzzle of a machine gun on a pedestal above the rail, where it could sweep the deck forward and aft, or be swung out to command the water.

Below, on the pier, a screaming mass of humanity eddied and swirled about the iron gates. There two English officers were running practiced hands over the bodies of every Chinese —women and children, as well as men—before they were admitted to the ship. Pigs, chickens, ducks, and geese, crammed into wicker baskets, added their individual protests to the babble of human voices. The moment a Chinese reached the deck, he pushed and fought his way to the most sheltered part of the ship and sat down. Spreading his belongings about him, he tried to pre-empt as much space as possible. As the crowd thickened, his personal territory gradually narrowed, but he protested every inch, screaming at the top of his lungs. It seemed that a mob battle would break out at any moment, but by the time the ship was under way the bedlam had subsided into friendly conversation. The passengers drank tea, which came from somewhere up forward, and exchanged amenities with their fellow squatters.

Before dinner Captain Beecher took Ken and Jack Benton over the ship. Every inch of the vessel was being searched, not only for weapons but for smuggled goods. Ken had a feeling that, with this efficient Englishman in command, neither pirates nor any catastrophe of the sea would keep the *Sunkiang* from her appointed destination.

IV. Capture of the "Sunkiang"

THE *Sunkiang* was large for a coastal vessel, with a comfortable saloon for dining and social activities. Benton and Ken had a small cabin well forward. The passengers were all Chinese, except for an Englishman, James Bryson, the editor of a Tientsin newspaper, and themselves. Bryson was well known throughout the Orient. He played no politics, was fearlessly honest, and was respected by Chinese and foreigners alike.

For two days the ship plowed through a calm sea, sometimes hardly a mile from shore. Ken never tired of watching the mass of humanity huddled on the open deck below him. Each family had made itself comfortable in a few yards of space. Domestic affairs continued as placidly as though they were ashore. The fact that their bodies were packed together like sardines in a box seemed only to add to the general happiness.

On the second day Ken noticed that every officer appeared with a .45-caliber revolver in a holster at his waist. The grille of the bridge was opened with care. The deck passengers gazed in curiosity, jabbering among themselves like a flock of starlings. No more harmless group of human beings could be imagined.

At four o'clock in the afternoon Ken stood on the upper boat deck alone, waiting to see the watch changed. Jack Benton was asleep in their cabin. The third officer had the bridge. His name was Balcom. He unlocked the grille and started down the ladder. Suddenly, out of the mass of sprawling Chinese, ten or fifteen coolies leaped to their feet with pistols in their hands. Some had knives too.

Four or five coolies clustered about the ladder as the mate came down. One of them yelled at him to put up his hands. Instead, he went for his gun. A pirate shot him behind the ear. His body rolled down the stairs onto the deck. Just then Captain Beecher opened his cabin door. In one motion he drew his revolver and fired at the man who had killed Balcom. The captain then ducked back into his cabin and out the other door on the port side. A running pirate crashed into him head on, and they both went down. The Chinese fired as he fell, but missed, and Beecher shot him through the body. Ken saw the captain scramble up and dash toward the bridge, but two men grabbed him from behind before he could use his gun. In a moment his arms and feet were tied up. The Chinese rolled him into the scuppers and ran up the bridge ladder. Hell broke loose all over the ship—men shouting, women screaming, and guns going off.

Ken slipped behind a canvas-covered lifeboat and flattened himself on the deck, where he was out of sight. He felt sick, and his brain was numb. Nothing of what was happening seemed real. In fifteen minutes the shooting stopped. A big, pockmarked Chinese appeared to be boss, and he started to clean up the ship. As a body was tossed over the bridge, Ken caught a glimpse of three gold stripes on the sleeve. That would be the first officer. Two more bodies went into the sea. He heard splashes on the starboard side too, but he couldn't tell whether they were ship's officers or dead pirates.

Finally the boss pirate came back to the captain, with two others. The pockmarked fellow reached down and yanked the captain out of the scuppers. He kicked him a couple of times and said something which Ken couldn't understand. The captain nodded. Then the boss pirate untied Beecher's legs and, with a pistol at his back, pushed him up the ladder into the chartroom. Pretty soon the engines started and the ship swung about. Ken guessed the pirates had complete control of the vessel but couldn't take her into Bias Bay themselves. That was why they hadn't killed the captain.

When the *Sunkiang* got under way Ken unlaced part of the canvas cover and slipped into the lifeboat. He felt sure he wouldn't be discovered there, for no one had come onto the top deck during the fight. He was beginning to get terribly scared, now that the action was over and he had time to think. He wondered what had happened to Jack. And what would the pirates do with the ship when they got to Bias Bay? Captain Beecher had said that after they had taken what they wanted of the cargo and passengers, they usually let the vessel go. Perhaps some of the Chinese were rich, and the pirates knew about them. One couldn't tell whether they were rich or not. They all wore gowns that looked alike. Anyway, there was nothing for him to do except stay there and wait for what might happen. That was the hardest part—just to wait!

Two hours before dark the *Sunkiang* reached Bias Bay. By lifting the cover a little, Ken could see a rocky shoreline with mud huts backed up against the hills. People were running along the beach. About twenty sampans (small boats) swarmed out from the village, and a lot of Chinese climbed aboard. He could hear them running about over all the decks. There was much noise, and some of the sampans went away, full of boxes and bales.

Ken was thirsty and hungry. He knew that every ship's boat was supposed to be stocked with food and water. In the stern he found a locker lined with water bottles on one side, and a dozen cans of hard biscuits. After eating, he felt better. It was getting dark in the boat. Before he knew it, he had dropped off to sleep.

The sound of the engines waked him. The ship was under way. He pulled up the cover and scrambled out of the boat. Lights of the village at Bias Bay were disappearing astern. Then he heard English voices. The pirates must have left the ship.

Ken ran down the ladder to the main deck. Dozens of frightened Chinese were huddled together among their chickens and ducks. He pushed his way to the bridge ladder. At the top he saw Benton and James Bryson. With a shout of joy, Jack ran down and threw his arms about Ken.

"Thank heaven you're alive! We thought you'd been killed and tossed over the side. Where were you?"

"In the lifeboat on the top deck. What happened to you?"

"The pirates kept us in the main cabin. They searched everybody for money and jewelry, but no one was harmed, even though they were pretty rough."

The captain and the second officer came out of the charthouse. They gave Ken a warm greeting.

"Now all the cabin passengers are accounted for," Captain Beecher said. "We were afraid you'd been done in. It's a bad show—a very bad show. I can't think where they had their weapons hidden. Must have bribed some of the crew to bring them aboard. But we'll find out."

"What happened to you, Captain?" Bryson asked.

"When the first gun went off I ran out of my cabin, just as poor Balcom's body rolled down the bridge ladder. I shot the fellow who killed him and then tried to get up to the bridge from the other side, but two of them caught me from behind. They tied me up and left me in the scuppers on the port side.

"After things quieted down, the boss pirate came back to me with a couple of others. I thought my number was up. I only hoped they'd untie me before they chucked me overboard, but I was sure they wouldn't. Instead, they said I wouldn't be killed if I took the ship into Bias Bay. Fortunately, I can understand Cantonese. Of course I agreed.

"In the chart room they told me to lay a course for Bias Bay and ring for full speed ahead. I wondered if the engines would answer, but they did right away. The pirates had men in every key point on the ship.

"When we got there the boss pirate ordered me to anchor in that cove. Then they tied my hands again and took me into my cabin. I didn't know how many of our officers were alive, but pretty soon the chief engineer was pushed in. A little later they brought the purser and the wireless operator with the second mate. He told me the second engineer and the first and third mates had been killed. I knew about the last two already. The purser said they had made him open the safe, and that the passengers had been searched for money.

"We all thought the pirates would sink the ship with us on it. But a little while ago the boss pirate came in and made a speech. He said we were to take the *Sunkiang* out of Bias Bay and get going fast. We didn't believe him, even when they untied us—thought we'd surely be shot. But the whole crowd climbed into sampans and went ashore. That's the story up to now. There'll be hell to pay when we get to Hong Kong."

"What," Bryson asked, "was the reason they picked on you this trip? Did you have any special cargo?"

"As a matter of fact, we did have, but I'm sure it is gone now. We were carrying the largest consignment of ginseng and of deer antlers that has come down from Manchuria in years. I suppose it was worth a quarter of a million dollars. Also there were about one hundred thousand dollars in the safe. Our pockmarked pirate and his friends made a rich haul."

"What is ginseng?" Ken asked. "And why should deer antlers be valuable?"

Captain Beecher smiled. "Jack will give you all the scientific details, but as an old China hand I can say ginseng is a root found in North China, Manchuria, and Korea, and that the Chinese believe it has wonderful medicinal qualities. They think it will cure almost anything and give extraordinary vigor and long life, particularly if the root is shaped like a man. It's very rare and valuable. Deer antlers in the 'velvet' are potent medicine too. The Chinese grind them up and make a tonic that sells for a high price."

Bryson, a good newspaperman, had been taking notes as the captain gave his account. He stuffed them in his pocket with an air of satisfaction.

"Well, I've certainly got the story of this piracy at first hand," he said. "Wait until you read what I write about this affair in the *Peking–Tientsin Times!* It's a disgrace that such a thing could happen to a British ship within a few miles of a British colony. The Chinese ought to be made to pay a handsome indemnity for the men who have been killed. But," he added with a sigh, "I suppose it will all fizzle out in diplomatic notes and talk. Probably some high Chinese officials are behind it. They'll all get their share of the loot."

The morning sun was shooting long shafts of light over the hills as the *Sunkiang* nosed her way into the most picturesque harbor in the world. Hong Kong lay before them like a glittering jewel. The "Peak" rose steeply from within the little city, dotted with hundreds of houses clinging to its almost perpendicular sides, amid a smothering of vegetation. Ken stood beside Jack Benton at the rail. The beauty of the shoreline, the strange odors drifting across the water, and the bat-winged junks slipping quietly past the ship like sailing ghosts made him feel that he was about to enter a new world.

On the way down from Bias Bay the radio operator had put the ship's wireless in working order. The captain sent a message to the *Sunkiang's* agents, telling briefly what had happened. When the vessel dropped anchor, newspaper reporters arrived with the American consul and other officials. All the passengers and ship's officers were interviewed. None of the Chinese crew was allowed ashore until an investigation as to how the pirates had obtained their weapons had been completed by the harbor police. At the end of the day both Ken and Jack were exhausted. Never had they been happier to go to bed.

V. A Rope's End
for the Pockmarked Pirate

WHEN Ken woke next morning he wondered where he
was. Then memory reached into his sleep-fogged mind.
Hong Kong! This was the Astor Hotel! The room was enormous and bare—furniture of the Victorian era; red-tiled floor;
no rugs; a huge electric fan in the ceiling. Jack Benton slept in
the other bed, one arm across his face. Ken looked at his watch.
It was only six-thirty, but he couldn't go back to sleep. Visions
of what had happened on the *Sunkiang* had danced through

his dreams like fluttering wraiths. He wanted to be rid of them and to explore this strange bit of England in the Orient.

He slipped out of bed and stepped across the floor and through the French windows to the wide balcony outside the room. The hotel was one of a line of foreign-style buildings, much like those in the business centers of Yokohama and Shanghai. Rickshaws rolled on rubber tires along the street, and a diminutive brown pony pulling a low, open carriage clop-clopped over the pavement. An air of order and dignified quiet pervaded the scene—British to the core; very, very British. But then, ludicrously incongruous, Ken saw a great bearded Sikh policeman solemnly driving in front of him four sheepish Chinese coolies, the ends of their pigtails tied together in a single knot. He roared with laughter. That couldn't be London or New York or anywhere else in the world but China! As Ken turned back into the room Benton opened his eyes, stretched, and yawned.

"What time is it?"

"Only six-thirty. Sorry I waked you, but I couldn't sleep."

"Time to be up and doing. Business starts early here in the heat, and most people rest for two or three hours during the middle of the day. Ring for breakfast, will you, please?"

On the way to Hong Kong Benton had made a list of supplies for their Yunnan expedition. He used the system of the unit food box. Each case was packed to weigh seventy pounds and contained all the necessary staple supplies for two persons for ten days; thus, only one box need be opened at a time, and if they separated there would be no bother of repacking. Flour, rice, butter, tea, sugar, coffee, milk, bacon, and marmalade made up the bulk of their supplies. Fruit, vegetables, meat, and eggs they could obtain in plenty until they entered the unexplored country beyond Chinese civilization.

At Lane and Crawford, one of the great stores of the Orient, an assistant manager took over their problem. In his efficient hands, it became no problem at all. Benton simply gave him specifications for the boxes and their contents and said they must be ready in four days, for Ken and he were sailing for Haiphong, Indochina, on the S.S. *Haitan*. The boxes would be ready, the manager said. All other equipment—silk tents, guns, ammunition, traps, and collecting gear—Benton had brought with him from New York. The men were left to explore the little island at their leisure.

Ken liked Hong Kong. Nestling at the foot of the green-clothed Peak, it had the intimacy of a small town in spite of the veneer of British officialdom and rigid custom. In the harbor one could count the flags of almost every maritime nation of the world on freighters, tramp steamers, or great passenger liners, with a sprinkling of ships of war. The boat city fascinated him. There thousands of Chinese lived and died on medieval-looking junks and sampans, packed together as closely as sardines in a box. This was the Hong Kong of pirates and smugglers, of romance, intrigue, and high adventure!

They lunched with the American consul at the club, where white-clad Britishers and a sprinkling of Americans drank their gin and bitters at a long bar and exchanged news of the day. They were introduced to a dozen men who wanted to hear the story of the piracy at first hand.

The second morning an invitation to dinner at Government House came from Sir George and Lady Allen-Thorpe. There were no other guests that night.

"Hope you don't mind this family party," the governor said, "but I've done a bit of traveling in Yunnan, and I'm interested in your expedition. Couldn't talk with you if we had a lot of people. I know you're tired of telling about the piracy on the *Sunkiang*, and I've read all the official reports. So I'll let you off that. Now this idea of capturing a snow leopard alive fascinates me! Good show if you can do it. Pretty difficult. No white man has shot one. Several of our chaps from India have had a go at it but never even saw one. The beasts live right up at the snowline in devilish rough country. Suppose you know all that, of course."

Benton smiled. "We're not betting too much on getting one alive, but I think there is a good chance if we stay long enough. None of your officers from India had unlimited time; they were always on specified leave. Moreover, they wanted some other shooting and couldn't get it if they worked on just one beast. At least that's the way it seemed to me from the published accounts I've read."

"That's true. Maybe you'll pull it off. You Americans have a way of getting what you want. I suppose you'll rely on native hunters?"

"Yes, I always do. Some of them are really good. Even though snow leopards are rare, a few skins do find their way every year to markets in China, and the natives must have trapped them. If we have the right people I see no reason why we can't capture one eventually. Of course, taking it out of the mountains to the coast is another matter. We'll have to face that when we've caught the beast. But the purpose of the expedition isn't just to get a snow leopard. We want to explore the country and study its zoology."

"Yes, I know that, and you couldn't be doing a more exciting or worth-while job. As far as natives are concerned, the Mosos are your best bet. I hunted with them several times, and of all the aborigines in Yunnan they seem most reliable. Some of them are really fine men. You'll see dozens of different tribes in the northwest. You know, of course, that as the Chinese came in, thousands of years ago, they gradually pushed the aboriginal natives back into that corner of the province. There is no more interesting part of the world for an anthropologist. Some of the tribes have only a few individuals left, and they are living in the wildest mountains."

Benton sighed. "I know that Ken and I will feel awfully ineffectual when we see so many important problems that we can't touch. Neither of us knows much about anthropology, and even if we did it wouldn't do much good. It's a lifetime job for a trained man. Someday a chap will come along and dedicate himself to studying the racial problems of this part of the world. No one knows, even yet, just where the Chinese originally came from."

So the talk went on until late in the evening. When they rose to leave, the governor said, "I'd give almost anything to go with you, but I'm tied to this job for some years yet. If you get into any jam with the Chinese where I could be of use, I'd be happy to help. Never can tell what will happen. Good luck to you."

After leaving Government House, the men walked down the quiet street in the soft tropic night. The lights of a hundred ships winked seductively from the dark waters of the bay.

Ken had never felt less like going to bed. "This place fascinates me," he said. "I wish we could have a look at some of the night life. It must be exciting. I feel so much is going on that one never sees in the daytime. I hate to miss anything."

"Well, why not? I'm not sleepy either. Let's drop in at the club. Maybe we'll find someone there who knows more about it than I do."

Captain Beecher was in the lobby. He greeted them warmly. "I've been wanting to see you to say good-by, but I've been tied up in the investigation about the *Sunkiang*. It's not ended yet."

"Have you any idea who got the pistols aboard for the pirates, and how they did it?"

"Not definitely, but it looks very much as though the Tientsin comparador—the Chinese contractor for supplies—had a hand in it. We'll find out eventually, I think. The only trouble is that it may lead to some Chinese officials who are too high up to touch. That cargo of ginseng and deer antlers was a pretty big temptation to any Chinese. They'd rather have ginseng than gold any day. I doubt if we'll ever get an indemnity for the chaps who were killed. The insurance company stands to lose their shirts."

After half an hour's talk Jack said, "Ken wants to get a glimpse of Hong Kong night life—not to participate, but just a look-see. I haven't been here for so long I don't know the ropes. Have you any suggestions?"

"Sure. Ship Street. It's the toughest place on the China coast, but also one of the most interesting and picturesque—sailors of every nationality in the world, having a binge; opium-smoking joints; cafés and drug shops; wine, women, and song! Still, it's what most of the China coast was like in the old days. I haven't been there in a year, and I'd like to go. Anyway, Ken ought to see it as a part of his Oriental education. But do you happen to have a gun on you, Jack? You never can tell what will happen on Ship Street."

Benton laughed. "Harry, do you suppose that when I dine with the governor of the Hong Kong Colony I carry a gun? And if I did, where would I conceal it in this tight little mess jacket?"

Captain Beecher grinned sheepishly. "I forgot you'd been up to Government House."

"We'll stop at the Astor, and Ken and I can heel ourselves. We've a couple of little .32-caliber automatics that don't make much of a bulge. Also we'll get out of these monkey jackets into day whites."

"That will be good," Beecher said. "You do look pretty conspicuous. The people you'll see down there don't wear evening clothes—at least not that kind."

Ken felt a thrill of excitement as they left the hotel and took rickshaws through a maze of dark alleys toward the typhoon harbor. Back from the waterfront, out of the entrance to a narrow street, came a hum of strange sounds and a glare of lights. The men paid off the rickshaws and walked into another world.

Signs painted black, with picturesque Chinese characters in gold, swung from gilded balconies; yellow banners and streamers of red silk crossed the street high above the men's heads; paper images of grinning Chinese gods and dragons glared from the fronts of drug shops where strange objects were displayed for sale. On one counter Ken saw a red-banded snake, half swallowed by another, floating in a jar of white liquid; scorpions and dried lizards strung by their tails like beads on a long string; shriveled bats with wings outspread; a human skull; and a flute made from the legbone of a bandit, so the legend said.

Halfway down the street, out of the door of a Chinese theater, came a wail of high-pitched fiddles, then the boom of drums and a clash of cymbals. The subtle smell of burning incense and the barbaric music were like an intoxicating drink that inflamed the senses but dulled the brain.

In and out of the open-faced bars swirled and eddied the most polygot crowd of human beings one could find at any port on earth. Portuguese, French, Spanish, Italian, English, Dutch, and American sailors, some of them drunk, sang at the

tops of their voices as they staggered in uncertain waves down
the street. Malays, their lips streaked with red betel nut, Fili-
pinos, Japanese, and turbaned Indians, Manchu Tartars, and
merchants from far Turkestan, drank and ate and gambled
with Chinese in long silk gowns. Women, brilliant in tawdry
finery and with painted faces, waved their hands and called to
the men in the surging mass below their balconies.

Ken was fascinated. In its kaleidoscopic mass of life and
color the street seemed like some pageant on the stage of a
theater. It was difficult to realize that this was reality; that it
went on night after night and had gone on for unnumbered
years; that he, Ken Lewis, was a living, breathing actor in this
strange drama of the Orient. He walked between Captain
Beecher and Jack Benton, grateful for the confidence that the
two men gave him.

Near the end of the street a wave of laughter and singing
swept out of a café. "Let's go in and see what gives," the captain said. "It sounds like a fun place."

They stepped inside a door, which was separated from the
street only by half a dozen vertical wooden bars, lacquered
with green and gold. There, in the middle of the room, stood
the pockmarked boss of the *Sunkiang* pirates and two others.
Dressed like Chinese gentlemen—silk gowns and all the rest—
they were buying drinks for everyone in the place, just throwing money about. The captain knew them instantly, and they
recognized him just as quickly. All three were pretty drunk,
but they had sense enough to make a break for the door.

"Never," said Captain Beecher afterward, "did I have more
gratification than when my fist smashed onto that big brute's
ugly mouth. I gave him everything I had, and he went down
like a felled ox."

Benton knocked out another. The third pirate drew a gun,

but he had no time to use it. Ken grabbed his arm and landed an uppercut that started from his waist and traveled upward with all his weight behind it. His fist caught the pirate on the chin and lifted him off his feet. The man slumped to the floor, out as cold as a dead herring.

Some of the Chinese in the café ran into the street, yelling for the police; but before the police arrived the three pirates were trussed up like pigs ready for market. Captain Beecher superintended the tying. As he rolled the boss pirate over on his face, he said with enormous satisfaction, "This, my lad, is what you did to me. But you kicked me, too. That I shall not do, for I won't soil my shoes. But I'll be there to watch you hang."

All of the pirates were loaded with money and were wearing rings and watches from the *Sunkiang* passengers. Evidently they had thought they were safe, dressed as they were. They had come down from Bias Bay to spend some of their loot in the hot spots of Hong Kong, just as the old-time pirates used to do in New Orleans and the cities along the Caribbean coast. There was little chance that anyone would have recognized them if Captain Beecher had not happened to be in Ship Street that night.

When the police had taken the pirates in charge, Benton remarked to the captain, "I guess Ken has seen enough for one night. I know I have. It's almost two o'clock. I suggest that we go home."

"Right you are, and I don't mind saying it has been one of the most profitable evenings I've ever spent. Now we'll find out who put those pistols on the *Sunkiang* and where they were hidden. You can be sure the harbor police will sweat the truth out of those gentlemen before daylight."

Captain Beecher was right. The pirates made a full confession. As had been suspected, the Chinese comparador in Tientsin was at the bottom of the plot. When he heard of the ginseng and deer antlers that were consigned to Hong Kong, he got in touch with the pirates at Bias Bay. They boarded the ship in Foochow as Jack and Ken had done. One of the comparador's carpenters made some minor repairs in the forecastle while the ship was tied up to the wharf in Tientsin. He loosened a plank in the wall behind the quartermaster's bunk. The space was large enough to hold twenty-five pistols and ammunition. The quartermaster, bosun, and half a dozen members of the crew were in the plot. At various times they brought the guns to the ship while others of the crew were ashore in Tientsin. The day after the ship left Foochow they began bringing up the pistols, two or three at a time, and arming the pirates.

The pockmarked pirate said he was in command only of operations on the ship. After it reached Bias Bay another man had taken charge of the cargo. He protested that he knew nothing about where it had gone, except that it had been shipped out the same night. Doubtless its distribution was handled by one of the big Chinese merchants in cahoots with the officials—which one probably never would be discovered.

The quartermaster, bosun, and six members of the *Sunkiang* crew joined the pirates in jail before morning dawned in Hong Kong. Tientsin's harbor police were notified by radio. They arrested the comparador and several of his men who were implicated in the plot. Altogether, it proved to be the most wholesale and satisfactory cleanup of pirates and their accomplices that had happened in the colony for years. And, as Jack Benton remarked to Ken, "It all came about because you weren't sleepy after leaving Government House and wanted to see a little of Hong Kong night life."

Two days after the Ship Street episode Ken Lewis and Jack Benton boarded the S.S. *Haitan,* bound for Haiphong on the coast of Indochina. With them was Wu Hung-tao, an English-speaking Chinese from Shanghai who for five years had lived in Yunnan; also Ching, a cheerful, spry little Pekinese cook.

"We are lucky to get Wu," Benton said. "I had him in Fukien three years ago, and as soon as I arrived in China he asked if I'd take him with us. He is a real jewel. He gave up a fine job, but he considers it his duty. As long as I continue to come to China he'll be ready to go anywhere with me, at any time. That's typically Chinese. They are a wonderful people. You'll get to love them, as I do."

The *Haitan* was much like the *Sunkiang,* with the same steel grille around the bridge and a machine gun in each corner. The officers all carried revolvers.

"Not much danger from pirates after we get out of Hong Kong waters," the captain said, "but we never take chances."

The ship dropped anchor off the island of Hainan for a brief stop, but no one went ashore. Benton pointed to the dim outlines of a mountain far back from the beach.

"That's called the Five Fingers, Ken, and it has never been explored by white men. The natives are a bad lot—head-hunters—and the valleys reek with a deadly malaria, but some-day you and I are going there. It can be done if we prepare properly and get introductions to the hill people as we go along. It's worth doing. Almost everything we'd get zoologi-cally would be new to science, and we'd probably find some extraordinary species. No white men live on the island except a few missionaries, and they don't venture far from the coast. One of them did go into the hills but never returned. Three months later a friendly native brought his dried head to the mission station."

At Haiphong, Benton and Ken got their equipment aboard the French railroad that runs through the steaming tropical jungle of Annam to Yünnanfu. From the car window they glimpsed a herd of brown monkeys in a dead tree, jumping up and down and waving their arms at the train like a crowd of children.

"This," Benton said, "is one of the greatest game countries in the world. It crawls with tigers, and a friend of mine shot an elephant within a few miles of the railroad. But the heat is awful, and the jungle is a sink-hole of fever. Personally, I wouldn't like it."

Yünnanfu, however, was a very different place. High up in the mountains beside a beautiful lake, the little city had the gaiety and charm of an Oriental summer resort where the heat-ridden French officials and their families came to find new life in the fresh, clear mountain air.

The British consul arranged a meeting with the Minister of Foreign Affairs of the Yunnan government. The fat little official seemed unhappy about the proposed expedition. The province, he admitted reluctantly, was overrun with bandits, who were completely beyond control of the few soldiers in the interior towns. If the Americans insisted on going, he told the consul, they must sign a paper releasing the government from responsibility for their safety. No indemnity could be demanded if they were killed or captured. Nevertheless, he would furnish four soldiers from the *yamen*, who would accompany the expedition to Tali-fu, the largest interior town. When Benton assured the minister that they were quite willing to sign the release, the official brightened considerably and toasted their success in glasses of sweet, warm champagne.

On the morning of departure from Yünnanfu, four soldiers arrived, armed with antique rifles and a strange assortment of cartridges. Not one of them fitted the guns.

"These fellows," Benton said, "will be about as much use as four newly born babies. However, there is nothing we can do about it. We have to pay each of them a dollar a day in advance, which will go into the pocket of the Minister of Foreign Affairs. That's his squeeze."

Thirty diminutive ponies loaded with equipment strung out in a wavering line along the lake shore when the expedition started. Benton and Ken rode in advance, Ken's long legs almost touching the ground on either side of his mount. Nevertheless, the little beasts moved off determinedly under the mountains of baggage piled on their backs.

The days drifted by in a succession of pleasant intervals. The inns were indescribably filthy and swarming with vermin, so at night they camped in temples. Ken couldn't understand that at first. "Imagine how we'd feel if some Chinese camped in one of our churches!"

Benton smiled. "It isn't the same thing at all. The Chinese don't have the profound religious feeling for their temples that we have for our churches. As a matter of fact, the belief in their various gods is basically more superstition than what we understand as religion. It is a sort of give-and-take business. They build a temple to keep their particular god in good humor; otherwise he'd cause trouble, give them bad crops, drought, floods, disease, or other calamities. They use the temples for all sorts of purposes not connected with religion. If we throw a few coppers in the collection box in front of the altar and give the caretaker a dollar, he'll be more than happy."

They set up their camp cots at the feet of huge gilded idols who grinned down at them benevolently, or on a stone porch under the stars. Ken liked the temples. He wrote in his journal:

Sometimes they stand in the midst of a populous town and we ride through long streets between dirty houses, swarming with ragged men and women and screaming children. Suddenly we come to the entrance of a temple, pass through a courtyard, close the huge gates, and are in another world. There is an inexpressible charm about the temples, lying asleep, as it were, among the trees of their courtyards, with stately pillared porches and picturesque gables upturned to the sky. They seem so very, very old and filled with such great calm and peace.

We leave early in the morning and ride off at the head of the caravan, followed by a straggling line of mules and ponies picking their way over the jagged stones of the road. We are seldom on level ground, for ten per cent of the entire province is mountainous, and I lose count of the ranges we have crossed.

Every morning the peaks about us are shrouded in fog. Sometimes the veil-like mists still float about the mountain tops when we climb into them and we are suddenly enveloped in a wet, gray blanket which sends us shivering into the coats tied to our saddles.

Jack and I walk a good deal. Skirting the edges of rice paddies, we pick up pheasants, ducks, and sometimes a goose with our shotguns. The food is wonderful. We can buy mushrooms of every size, from tiny things no bigger than the end of my finger, to great flat mushrooms as large as pancakes. One of these makes a full meal. Apples and persimmons and water-pears, eggs and chickens and pork are in all the markets. Jack says we had better eat our fill now, for when we get into the northern mountains, away from Chinese civilization, there won't be any of these things. So far, we have hardly touched our food boxes.

It seemed incredible that there could be any threat of tragedy and sudden death in this peaceful countryside, yet at every town, as they pushed deeper into the interior, stories of brigands became more prevalent. Caravans were being attacked, small villages raided, and people killed if they tried to defend their property.

"I don't like it," Benton said. "We'll be lucky if we get to Tali-fu without trouble."

"Suppose we are attacked on the road. What will we do, Jack?"

"It'll depend upon circumstances. If we're ambushed and they get us cold there's nothing we *can* do, but if there's half a chance we'll fight. Do you agree?"

"Of course. If they captured our caravan the expedition would be ended before it began. That would be terrible."

"I knew you'd say that, Ken, but I don't propose to get ambushed. Our soldiers are good for only one thing—as scouts. We'll send them a couple of hours ahead to talk with the villagers and travelers on the road. If there are bandits in any number in the vicinity, they'll hear of them and we'll make our plans. I'll give Wu a rifle and a pistol. He's a pretty fair shot. Ching can't shoot, but he has plenty of nerve and he won't leave us. They are the only ones we can depend upon. The *mafus*"—horsemen—"will run like rabbits if they think they can save their skins. You can't blame them. After all, they are hired only to care for the animals, and why should they risk being killed in our behalf?"

That night they camped in a temple at the foot of a mountain range. Their cots were on the open porch. Ken looked up at the stars for a long time. He couldn't sleep, for a medley of thoughts raced through his mind. He had known when he left New York that this sort of thing might happen. But then it had seemed romantic and glamorous—only an adventure, the sort of thing that was supposed to happen to explorers. Jack often said he didn't want adventures, for they disrupted work, but one couldn't always avoid them, no matter how carefully one prepared. Ken knew Benton wouldn't take foolish chances, but neither would he turn back. He wasn't that sort of man.

Ken wondered how he'd act if someone were shooting at him. He'd be scared green; of that he was certain. But he would never let Jack down—he'd rather die a hundred times. He loved his father and his mother, but he worshiped Benton. It wasn't the same thing at all. Never would he forget what Jack had said when Ken killed his first tiger—"Boy, I'm proud of you!" That had been the greatest moment of his life.

But could he bring himself to shoot a man? Would he ever forget it if he did? When he saw those men killed on the *Sunkiang* it had made him sick and weak all over. But suppose he were in a war? Then he'd have to kill men. If bandits attacked their caravan it would be just the same as war. He kept repeating that to himself, and it gave his troubled mind some peace. At last he went to sleep.

VI. Bandits on the Hilltop

AT BREAKFAST Benton talked to the soldiers. They were
to start at once up the road, stopping at every village
to inquire about bandits and question all the travelers. If they
had definite news two of them were to ride back at full speed
and report to him. Immediately the soldiers trotted out of the
temple compound on their ponies, clattering the rifle bolts to
strengthen their already failing courage.

Wu strapped on the big Colt revolver and handled his rifle
with assurance. Ching, the cook, seemed crestfallen when
Benton did not issue him a gun, but after the meal he slipped

out of the temple gate into the bazaar and returned with a large package wrapped in red paper. His air of mystery intrigued Ken.

"You seem awfully pleased with yourself, Ching. What have you got in that bundle?"

The cook grinned. "Me no tell, but this better than gun. Maybe *tui-fei* [bandits] come. Ching show you then." Ken had to let it go at that.

All morning the caravan climbed steadily up a steep mountainside, reaching the brow of a ridge only to find another and higher summit rising against the sky. The country below them spread out like a great green relief map. The clear air gave a wonderful sense of exhilaration and freedom, and Ken's spirits soared.

"I don't think we're going to have trouble, Jack," he said. "We haven't seen a sign of bandits."

Benton couldn't agree. "That doesn't mean a thing. The *mafus* tell me that the other side of the mountain is cut with deep canyons, and that's where *tui-fei* will wait for us if we're going to be attacked. They wouldn't bother us here in the open. Most of the caravans have been held up in that broken country, as near as I can find out. I understand there is a walled inn at the very summit of the pass, and I'm going to camp there. We ought to reach it about three o'clock; then we'll have a full day to go through the bad area."

The words were hardly out of his mouth when two of their soldiers came clattering down the trail in a cloud of dust and gravel.

"*Tui-fei!*" They gasped. "*Tui-fei*, many *tui-fei!*"

"How many?" Benton asked.

"A hundred. Maybe more. They wait in the hills a mile beyond the inn."

The men were almost incoherent from fright, but at last Benton got the story. A fuel-gatherer had suddenly come over a high ridge and seen the bandits lying among the rocks where the trail cut through a narrow canyon. He had dropped his pack and run back to the inn.

Benton lost no time in talk. "Ken, you and I will scout ahead on either side of the road. Wu, you keep the caravan moving as fast as it can go. We've got to get to the top of the pass in a hurry. It's only about three miles, the soldier said. I hope the bandits didn't see that woodcutter."

In less than an hour the pack train pushed through the gate of the mud-walled inn. Two other caravans were there. The compound seethed in a state of indescribable confusion. Shouting *mafus*, mules, and ponies crowded together, kicking and yelling.

At last Benton found the woodcutter who had discovered the bandits. Had the *tui-fei* seen him? No, he thought not. He had been on a ridge above the road and as soon as he glimpsed them lying among the rocks he had dropped his pack and run. How many *tui-fei*? He didn't know, but "many tens." That was all he had to offer.

Jack and Ken got themselves a pot of tea in the inn's kitchen.

"The only thing to do," Benton said, "is to wait and see what happens. When we don't appear on the road, the bandits will know we have stopped here. Their scouts may have been following us for days. If it is a large band they'll attack the inn tonight, for they will know we've been warned. I don't believe they'd risk it unless they have at least fifty men."

"What's your plan, Jack?"

"We have three rifles. You will take one side of the wall; I'll guard another and put Wu on the third. Ching can watch the fourth side. He doesn't know one end of a gun from the other but he's not scared. Did you see that grin on his face? He acts as though this were a picnic. I'm going to talk to the *mafus*. They have complete confidence in foreigners. All they need is leadership. If by chance the bandits get inside the walls the *mafus* will fight, all right. They don't want to lose their goods and animals any more than we do."

Jack went out into the bedlam of the compound. Standing on a pile of saddles, he clapped his hands until there was reasonable quiet. Then he began to speak.

"We are all travelers on the road together. We value our lives and we value our goods. We do not intend that *tui-fei* shall have them. They need not rob our caravans, or kill any of us, if we work together. We have rifles—good rifles—and we can shoot better than any *tui-fei*. We do not know how many bandits wait in the pass, but if there are many tens they will attack the inn tonight. I think we can keep them out, but if they get within the walls you must fight. Arm yourselves with whatever you can find. Will you all help?"

A murmur of approval ran through the crowd like wind in the dry leaves of an oak tree. "You have spoken well. We'll fight. Yes, we'll fight." Staves, carrying poles, scythes, and an ancient trident-spear appeared like magic from rooms and corners of the inn. The peasants brandished their weapons, jabbed the air, and whirled their staves, shouting curses at an imaginary enemy, working themselves up to a fever of courageous excitement. Suddenly the turmoil subsided. The *mafus* separated into groups and squatted on their heels to drink tea and smoke their pipes.

After dinner Ken and Benton sat on a corner of the wall, looking over the valley. The inn occupied the flat summit of a low, isolated peak. It was a perfect place for defense except that the ground in front of the walls was strewn with rocks and boulders. Dodging from one to another, a man could approach within a few yards without exposing himself except momentarily. To the east the white line of the road by which they had come wound like a gigantic snake up the wide valley to the inn. On the other side it dropped steeply into the black depths of a tortured mountain slope cut into a chaos of ravines and gullies by the knives of wind and frost and rain.

"That," said Benton, "is where our little friends are waiting. What a place for an ambush! They realize by this time that we're not coming through tonight. I wonder what they are doing now?"

"Probably trying to decide whether to rush the inn or lie doggo until morning," Ken replied. "The moon will be up a little after dark. That'll be good for us. Last night I couldn't sleep for a long time, and the moon was so bright I could see the lines in the palm of my hand. We can shoot all right."

"If they attack, Ken, they'll mean business. It will be our lives or theirs, for we've elected to fight to save our caravan— and, incidentally, these other poor people in the inn. I hope you won't feel too unhappy about bumping off a Chinese bandit if you have to."

"No, I won't. I thought it all out last night. It's just like war. If I were in the Army I wouldn't be any use unless I tried to kill some of the enemy. That's what these people are. I'll hate it, but it can't be helped."

Jack knocked the ashes out of his pipe. "Glad you've figured it that way. It's pretty sensible." Then, with a laugh, "I'll be awfully sorry for a *tui-fei* if you line your sights on him. I'd give a lot if I could shoot half as well as you do." He slipped off the wall. "Let's make the rounds and get posted. It will be dark in half an hour, and the *tui-fei* might come up before the moon rises."

Wu was already at his side of the wall, where he could see well down the valley. Opposite him the cook had built a throne of saddles on which he sat comfortably, smoking a cigarette. He grinned happily as Benton approached. "I all ready, Master," he said. "No *tui-fei* get over here."

"How are you going to stop them, Ching? They won't run just because you shout and wave your arms."

"You no make worry, Master. Ching fix 'em. You'll see."

"All right, but just the same you yell like the devil if you see anything out front. You've got good eyes, and I'm depending on you."

Ken's side of the wall overlooked the east. The gauze curtain of late evening gave place to the blackness of night. Almost imperceptibly the line of the road faded from sight. A great boulder, a hundred yards away, became only a dim shape; a dead tree on the lower slope stretched out bare arms like a man writhing in agony. In the east a streak of white light lay along the rim of a hill, and the edge of the moon pushed rapidly into the sky. On the great *kiang* (sleeping platform) of the inn a score of *mafus* were already snoring; others lay about the courtyard, their heads pillowed on saddles. With childlike faith that the foreigners would protect them, they had dismissed the thought of danger and were as sleepily content as though no bandits lurked almost at their door.

Ken rested his arms on the wall, his rifle beside him. Already the moonlight mottled the hill slope with white patches, intensifying the blackness of the rocks. He could see the great boulder silhouetted like a castle turret against the sky. Suddenly the darkness of the shadow seemed to deepen; then it lightened and darkened again, black upon black. That was movement. Ken strained his eyes.

Almost on the instant, Jack Benton's rifle tore the night

apart, sending waves of thunder crashing against the jagged ramparts, probing deeper and deeper into the inky blackness of the lower canyon. The boulder in front of Ken erupted like a volcano, spouting streaks of light. Bullets thudded into the walls and whined like angry bees above his head. A horse screamed—the terrible scream of an animal in mortal agony. For a moment stunned silence hung over the compound; then bedlam broke loose. Cursing men, screaming women, and crying children milled about in a hysterical mass. A dozen dark figures leaped to their feet in front of Ken, darting for the walls. Automatically he fired at the foremost man. The bandit flattened like a wet rag. Another almost reached the wall, only to roll in a screaming ball down the hill. Wu's rifle blazed fiercely at Ken's right, but he saw a man gain the wall and leap into the compound. Hardly had the bandit landed before a *mafu* swinging a carrying pole felled him like an ox.

Another scrambled over the parapet. Two brigands came at Ken, spitting curses. He had a momentary glimpse of bared teeth and an evil face as he pushed his rifle into the man's stomach and pressed the trigger. The second bandit dropped back over the wall and crouched against the base. His dead companion slumped down, almost on his head. A dozen bandits fought desperately in the compound, with clubbed guns, against a swarm of *mafus*. Ken dropped his rifle and drew his revolver as a second wave of black figures gained the walls.

Suddenly, off to his left, came a blinding flash of light and a shattering explosion. A moment later a tiny body ducked almost under his arm and threw an object streaming sparks into the night. It burst in mid-air, and the whole world seemed to end in a red blaze. The little man squealed like a rabbit, dashed to Wu's wall, and heaved another bomb into a mass of swarming *tui-fei;* then he scurried across the compound to where

Benton struggled with a huge Chinese. Just as Jack's fist crashed into the bandit's face, a tremendous explosion seemed to open the gates of Hell.

The battle ended as suddenly as it had begun. The bandits outside the walls scattered into the shadows like a covey of terrified quail; fourteen within the compound were overpowered, trussed with saddle ropes, and laid side by side. The infuriated *mafus* kicked and mauled them until Benton intervened. Ching stood at one side, grinning like a gargoyle.

"Cook, what on earth were those things you threw over the walls? Hand grenades?"

"No, Master, those belong firecrackers—big ones. You see." He produced a half-dozen giant cannon crackers, a foot long and six inches in circumference. "They not kill anybody, but they make terrible noise. Yesterday when you no give me gun, I catch 'em in bazaar. I think they do all right."

"I'll say they did all right! Ching, you're a wonder. You saved our lives. In another ten minutes the place would have been full of bandits. We couldn't have handled them all."

Benton turned to Ken. "Let's see how many people are hurt."

The two men made the rounds of the compound. Only one horse was dead, killed in the first volley by a ricocheting bullet. Inside the house a dozen *mafus* groaned on the *kiang*. Jack made a quick examination. Most of the wounds were bruises, but one man had a broken arm and another a fractured skull. Not one had been touched by a bullet.

After Jack had given the injured men first aid he said to Ken, "I've got to go outside and see if any of the bandits are alive. Want to come?"

"No, Jack, if you don't mind. I'm sort of weak inside. While the fight was going on I didn't feel anything—guess it was the excitement. When those bandits jumped out of the dark and rushed at me it was like when the black tiger charged us. I couldn't think they were men—just wild animals. I still don't realize they were human beings, and I don't want to see any bodies."

Jack put his hand on the boy's shoulder. "I understand just how you feel. That's the way to think of it. But I do want to say you did a swell job. Were you frightened?"

"No, I wasn't a bit. I was just furiously angry. I've heard about red patches flashing across your eyes, and that's just what I had—jagged red patches. It seemed so rotten that those people were trying to kill us when we hadn't done anything to them. But after it was over I got plenty scared. I still am."

"You weren't the only one, Ken. I did too. While it is going on you're too concentrated upon doing what you have to do, to think. It's afterward, when your imagination begins to work, that you get frightened. I'll tell Ching to make some tea while Wu and I go outside."

The bodies of eight Chinese lay not far from the walls. All of them were dead. With the help of a half-dozen *mafus* Benton and Wu dragged them behind a rock and covered the gruesome pile with a cloth from the inn.

"How many do you think they were, Mr. Benton?" Wu asked.

"Certainly a hundred, maybe more. At least twenty-five attacked my side of the wall."

"Yes, several tens came at me. I can't shoot so well as you and Mr. Lewis, and if Ching hadn't come just when he did they'd have surely killed me. When that big firecracker went off they ran like rats. So did I. It seemed like the end of the world."

The inn compound was alight with little fires at which the

mafus boiled tea and drank *kaoliang* wine. Some stretched comfortably and "cooked" opium pills over a flame. Inhaling the seductive fumes, they drifted off into the unreal world of the drug addict, where each one became the real hero of the fight.

All the caravans left together the next morning shortly after daylight. The mules and ponies strung out in a long line down the steep slope into the depths of the canyon. Benton had little fear of further bandit trouble, but until they emerged into a broad valley, green with rice paddies, he and Ken watched every rock and tree and reconnoitered side ravines. News of the battle had already reached Ching Cho, the first sizable town. There at the *yamen* (the official office of the province) Jack reported to the magistrate.

"You have rendered a great service," the man told them. "That band of *tui-fei* moved in here two weeks ago and has robbed a dozen caravans. I have asked for soldiers from the district governor at Tali-fu, but they haven't come. I'll send men to the inn to bring the prisoners. They will be executed at once. I hope you can be present."

Benton thanked the magistrate but said they must hurry on to Tali-fu.

When they were on the road again Ken asked, "What will they do with those bandits? Shoot them?"

"Probably not; more likely cut off their heads. It's a horrible spectacle, but strangely enough many tourists, when they come to China, ask to see an execution. Guess there's a morbid streak in everyone. That's the reason murder stories are so popular. But believe me, not many want to see a beheading more than once. I was present at one in Mukden, and I'll never forget it. I dreamed about it for weeks. Don't ever let your curiosity get the better of you as I did. You'll be sorry if you do."

"You can bet I won't. Strangely enough, I don't have any

feeling about that fight last night except that it was terribly exciting. I feel sort of ashamed that I'm not unhappy about it, but it seems just as though I'd been to a moving picture and that it wasn't real at all."

"Keep on thinking of it that way. It *was* like a movie, only we wouldn't be alive now if it hadn't been for Ching. Imagine that little chap thinking of firecrackers! Believe me, I'm going to keep some handy from now on. They're better than machine guns, for they don't kill anybody. But I'll bet some of those *tui-fei* nearly died of fright.

"We won't have any more bandit trouble after we leave Tali-fu, for they stick to the main roads, where there are caravans to rob. It will be five days' travel from Tali-fu to Li-chiang and that's where the big forests begin. There's a great mountain there—twenty thousand feet or more. A botanist, Jim Streter, who was plant-hunting for the United States Department of Agriculture, told me about it. He is the only one I know of who has been there. He says it's a wonderful place— full of game. What I'd like to do is to camp well up on the slopes and begin our collecting. Most of the small mammals, such as shrews and mice and rats, ought to be new to science. We'll hunt serow, goral, and bear. After that we'll strike north and west into new country and get up where the snow leopards live. We're going to have fun, and we'll be doing a good job too. That's what's so satisfying about a naturalist's life."

"If I had all the money in the world, Jack, I'd want to do the same thing we're doing now. I can't think of anything more wonderful."

VII. The Snow Mountain

LATE in the afternoon the caravan stumbled along a road
paved with rough stone blocks, toward Tali-fu. On the
right lay a beautiful lake dotted with the white sails of fishing
boats; on the left the Tsang Mountains stretched 14,000 feet
into the clouds. Near the city the slender shafts of three ancient
pagodas showed ghostlike against the sky. For fifteen hundred
years their benign influence has guarded the stone graves that
spread over the plain in countless thousands.

In the weakening light the grim walls of the ancient city
seemed to recede strangely, melting into the haze. A picturesque gate loomed, shadowy and unreal even as they passed

through its gloomy arch and clattered up the stone-paved street. Wu found a temple outside the walls for their camp, and next morning Benton sent their cards to the *yamen*.

"This is your first formal interview, Ken," he said, "and it will be a good lesson in Chinese etiquette. Later, on your own expeditions, you'll be dealing with officials continually, and it is most important to learn how to behave properly according to their standards. Otherwise you'll get nowhere. Their customs are very different from ours, and naturally they think theirs are the only right ones. They don't make allowances for ignorance.

"When we reach the *yamen*, a servant will walk through the courtyards in front of us, holding our calling cards high above his head and shouting our names. He will usher us into the reception hall, where the magistrate will be waiting. He will bow, while holding both his own hands. We must do the same. The Chinese do not shake hands with each other. He will seat us at his *left*—not his right—for the left is the place of honor in China.

"He will first ask our names and where we live; then how old we are, how many children we have, and if our families are well. He will inquire about our journey. All this is rigid custom. We think such personal questions are rude, but the Chinese consider them as showing polite interest in the visitor. After these preliminaries we can gradually get around to our business.

"Tea will be brought as soon as we arrive. We can sip ours, holding the cup in both hands, but our host won't touch his until he wants the interview to end. Then he'll raise his cup to his lips, and we'll have to leave immediately. It would be impolite to stay even if we had not finished our business. As we go out, the official will walk beside us through the courtyards, and at each gate we must implore him not to come so far, and say that we are unworthy of such honor. If he considers us of sufficient importance, he will follow right out to the street door. If we don't rank that high in his estimation, he'll stop at one of the inner gates."

"Gosh, it sounds silly, Jack. Do they always do it that way?"

"Yes, always, and remember that some of our customs seem just as silly to them. 'When in Rome, do as the Romans do' is a pretty good motto."

It happened exactly as Benton had predicted, except for an extra ceremony in the inner court, where soldiers presented arms as they passed.

"This," said Jack, "is for what we did to the bandits."

The magistrate was a pleasant-looking man of forty. Since Jack spoke excellent Chinese they needed no interpreter, but Ken had to guess at much of what was being said, although he was studying the language. Finally the mandarin leaned forward and spoke, his face lighting with interest.

For a moment Benton stared; then he suddenly burst into a violent fit of coughing. When he had recovered, he replied gravely, and, after a few minutes, the magistrate lifted his tiny teacup to his lips. Jack rose immediately. As they proceeded through each courtyard Jack begged their host not to go farther. But he continued to the outer gate, bowing deeply in farewell.

Ken was consumed with curiosity. "What on earth happened when you started coughing? I thought at first you were laughing."

"I was. I've heard plenty of Chinese exaggeration, but this is the limit. The magistrate said it was reported that our cook's firecrackers killed 'many tens' of bandits—that means about a hundred—and that bodies, torn to shreds, were strewn all over the hills. Can you beat that?"

Ken roared. "Does he really believe it?"

"Of course he does. He asked me if I wouldn't give him some of our bombs to arm his personal guard. I told him we had only a few left and we needed them ourselves for other *tui-fei*. But Ching really did something for us. When that tale has been repeated a few more times we'll have killed a thousand bandits. It will be all over the province in a week or two, and we won't have any more trouble from *tui-fei*, you can be sure of that."

"But won't the cook give it away?"

"Not a chance. As a matter of fact, he really started the story. I heard him talking in the kitchen of the inn. He hinted that what had done the trick were some terrible bombs we had brought from America and had entrusted to him. He modestly admitted that he had saved the day, and, believe me, he did. Anyway, our permits are stamped, and we can get off tomorrow."

It was six days' travel to Lichiang. The country had begun to change. Villages were nonexistent. They rode through open pine forests and crossed a pass 10,000 feet high. As they came down into a marshy plain in the late afternoon, the outlines of a city wall were dimly visible against a fog-hung sky.

Lichiang proved to be a picturesque frontier town. Tibetans, great burly men wearing fur caps, long loose coats, and skin boots, swaggered along the streets in conscious arrogance. Each one carried a long sword and either a matchlock gun or a murderous-looking spear. Short, stocky Mosos and natives of half a dozen other tribes, with a few Chinese, made a fascinating picture. That night when the expedition camped in a temple on the summit of a hill beyond the town, Ken said to

Benton, "It is just like a circus. I can hardly wait to get back there tomorrow. Gosh, those Tibetans are wild-looking fellows. They certainly aren't much like Chinese. I'll bet firecrackers wouldn't make them run."

"You're dead right. They're a different breed of cats. They know how to take care of themselves. But I don't think we will have any trouble from them. The only natives I really worry about are the Lolos. They hate the Chinese and have killed most of the few foreigners who went into their country. We'll skirt Lolo Land, and they stick pretty close to their own territory, except for raids outside when the Chinese have been bothering them."

"What do you mean, 'Lolo Land'? Doesn't all of this western country belong to the Chinese?"

"Theoretically it does, but the Lolos hold a big section in Szechuan Province. They are a strange people; some of them have features more like Caucasians than like Orientals. Up to now they've managed to keep everyone out of their territory. The Chinese sent several expeditions against them, but few of the soldiers got back alive. Two or three white men who went in there were killed. A good many Lolos live outside their country here in the mountains of Yunnan. They are said to be peaceful. Nevertheless, I'd just as soon not run into any of them. But we won't worry about that. I want to have a look at the market tomorrow. When we rode through I saw animal skins hanging in several shops. They ought to give us a good idea of what we'll find up here."

Benton was right. Lichiang is an important fur market, and they found natives, fresh from the mountains, bargaining with the Chinese dealers for the sale of their skins. Hides of bears with white V-shaped breast marks, skins of foxes, pandas, enormous brown flying squirrels, civets, serows, and gorals, hung in every shop along the street. But the most interesting skins were those of two magnificent snow leopards. A pleasant-looking Moso had them. Fortunately he could speak Chinese, and Jack drew him to one side for talk.

He was called Latunga, he said. All his life he had lived in this region, but sometimes he went far across the frontier into Tibet, because he liked to explore new country. He had just returned from such a trip. The snow leopards were very rare. No man had ever shot one so far as he knew. These two had been trapped in deadfalls baited with gray monkeys. The monkeys lived at snowline, and the leopards liked them better than any other meat.

Latunga seemed the answer to their prayer for a good hunter. "Would you like to go with us?" Benton asked. "I will pay you well in silver dollars."

The Moso looked up with frankly appraising eyes. "Money is of small importance," he said. "I hunt because I love to hunt. Never have I seen men like you. I have heard of them, but they have not come here. I do not know that we would be happy together in the mountains. We must have further talk. After I have sold my furs I will come to you. Where is your dwelling place?"

"I am camped in the Temple of the High-spirited Insects on the summit of the hill north of the city. Come when you wish, but please bring the snow-leopard skins. Those I wish to buy."

Latunga arrived that afternoon. He was a small man, dressed in a patched buckskin jacket and short trousers, with a little felt skullcap on his head. His brown face easily broke into a smile, and his frank wonder at the expedition's rifles and equipment was most appealing. But he had, too, a certain reserve and dignity that stamped him as something more than an ordinary native. Ken thought back to the words of the governor of Hong Kong: "The Mosos are your best bet. I shot with them several times, and of all the aborigines in Yunnan they are most reliable. Some of them are really fine men."

Latunga agreed to hunt with them for a time, at least. He suggested that they go to the Snow Mountain if they wanted serow, goral, and bear. He had left his pack of dogs in a village twelve miles away, and he knew of a beautiful meadow far up on the slopes of the peak, where they could camp.

During their two days in Lichiang a dense gray curtain of fog had shrouded the country, but on the third morning, in brilliant sunlight, they rode out of the temple courtyard into a new and dazzling world. Ken gasped in delight. "Jack, look! Isn't it wonderful?"

About the valley, encircling mountains, white almost to their bases, rose, ridge upon ridge, like the foamy billows of a mighty ocean. To the north, silhouetted against a vivid blue sky, towered the great Snow Mountain, its jagged peak splashed with shining gold where the sun touched its summit. Fleecy clouds formed and floated upward to lose themselves in the deep, snow-filled craters beside the glacier.

The mountain, lying so white and still in its cradle of dark green forest, was like the altar of a vast cathedral. For a time the men rode in silence. Then Ken said, "It seems as though organ music will swell out of that canyon at any moment and we'll hear voices singing—but they won't be human voices! I feel more religious now than I ever did in church."

"I do too, Ken. I understand why natives worship the sun and the mountains and the forests. Men can build a church, but only God could make the mountains. You can't get far away from Him when you live close to nature."

In the early afternoon they camped in a tiny temple nestled in a grove of spruce trees on the outskirts of a straggling village. Latunga disappeared, only to return an hour later with two other Mosos and a pack of mongrel dogs yapping at his heels. Most of the dogs were white, but one splendid tawny hound trotted ahead with conscious dignity.

"That," said Latunga proudly, "is Big Red. He is the leader, and no other dog is like him in all this country."

Ken gave the dog the back of his hand to smell. Big Red sniffed for a moment and then ran his nose up the boy's arm. Ken scratched him behind the ears. Red licked Ken's hand and lay down at his feet.

The Moso was delighted. "He likes you. You will be friends. Not often does he do that. He will hunt for you as well as for me."

Rather diffidently Latunga exhibited his weapon. It was a crossbow that shot wicked little poisoned arrows. On a target thirty yards away, he plunked four arrows within a three-inch circle. They were about a foot long and made of bamboo, sharpened to needle-like points. When hunting big game, he smeared them with a black paste that he carried in a small wooden box. Benton never learned what the poison was. Latunga said he didn't know. He bought it at a Chinese drug shop in Lichiang—the only place that had it.

"When you kill an animal with a poisoned arrow, doesn't it spoil it for meat?" Ken asked.

"No. We cut out the flesh near where the arrow went in. The rest of it is all right."

"How long before the poison works?"

"About the time it takes to light a pipe." That would be not more than five seconds.

"At what range do you shoot?"

"Not far. After running awhile, a goral or serow will back up against a rock and fight the hounds. We get there as fast as we can, for very often the animal kills more than one of the pack. It is difficult to find good dogs. We couldn't get much game in these mountains without them."

At daylight next morning Latunga led the caravan up a winding trail along the edge of a steep escarpment. Three thousand feet below, the roof of their temple gleamed in the sunlight, and herds of sheep and goats massed into moving patches on the brown plain. Suddenly the trail ended in a beautiful open meadow. Just above their heads the white peak of the mountain towered in overwhelming majesty.

"We'll camp at the far end," Latunga said. "A stream runs down from a snowbank right at the edge of the forest."

When Ken jumped from his horse his legs felt like leaden weights and he could hardly breathe. "What's the matter with me, Jack? I've never been like this before."

"Don't worry; it's the altitude. We're twelve thousand feet above sea level, and the air is thin. You'll be all right if you take it easy and move slowly."

"But look at Latunga. He's running about like a goat."

"Well, he was born in these mountains and he's used to it. Tonight we'll probably wake up gasping for breath, but that will end after a week or two. For a while we'll have to do everything like a slow-motion movie."

Ken never forgot that first evening in camp. They had dinner about the fire and smoked their pipes while the Snow Mountain turned crimson in the afterglow of the sun, and the somber mass of the forest lost itself in the shadows of night. Then suddenly a great round moon edged over the trees, flooding the meadow with silver light. They slept, breathing the perfume of the spruce trees, and felt the unseen presence of the mighty peak standing guard about their mountain home.

VIII. Hunting in the Clouds

THE insistent drum of rain on the tent awakened Ken at daylight. He stretched luxuriously, wriggling his toes in the soft fur of the sleeping bag. His mind hovered in the delightful realm of half-sleep, with the background of something pleasurable about to happen. A gust of wind parted the door flaps, bringing the wild, sweet smell of dripping leaves and sodden grass.

Water gurgled near his head. Stretching his arm beneath the tent, he touched the little river draining off the slanting roof into the ditch along the side. On his lips the wet tasted bittersweet. Somehow it made him think of the balsam pillow his mother had given him years ago. He had always carried it with him to school and to New York, as a link with the summer vacations in the Adirondacks. New York! Towering buildings closing in like walls, the odor of carbon monoxide, the blare of taxi horns, the throbbing pulse of the city!

It all seemed years ago and a million miles away! Well, it was ten thousand miles, and that was a lot! In between lay memories of the voyage across the Pacific—water incredibly blue, flying fish, lazy days in the sunlight, moonlight nights! And a girl about his own age, a girl with eyes sometimes green, sometimes tawny, sometimes gray; he never could tell the color, for they changed continually. Carol Whitehouse was her name. They had stood on the open boat deck one night when the stars seemed so low they could almost reach up and pick one out of the sky. She was on the way to join her father at the legation in Peking for the summer vacation; next fall she would go to Vassar. Carol told him how thrilled she was with the thought of seeing the Forbidden City where the Empress Dowager had pulled the strings that made diplomats dance on the stage of half the world; of sitting on the Tartar Wall to watch the sun go down over yellow-tiled roofs; of picnics at temples in the Western Hills. Her father had promised her all that! But why was he, Ken, going to the Orient?

Under the spell of the night, and their companionship alone on the great deck, he had talked of his ambitions as he seldom did. He told her that he had always wanted to be a naturalist and explore the far corners of the world. Jack Benton had given him the chance. The girl listened with wide-eyed, breathless interest. He remembered how she had crumpled her little handkerchief and tightened her hands when he spoke of Jack's adventures with bandits and strange beasts.

"Just think," she had said. "That's what you will be doing too! How wonderful!"

On the morning when he sailed from Shanghai for South China she came to the dock to say good-by. He hadn't expected her, and her coming made him very happy. She looked lovely in a white dress. As the ship slipped away into the river a flood of sunlight caught her hair, turning it to shining gold. That was the picture of her he always carried in his mind. He thought of her often, but he had never mentioned her to Jack. She was something very special, to be kept for himself alone. One thing he did know: when he returned to New York his first visit would be to Vassar College.

His thoughts shifted to his first hunting days in China—the tigress that had stood snarling at him on the rice dike, and the clawing black man-eater rolling at his feet in the half-light of the tropic night. Those memories were vivid and exciting. But of the pirates and the fight with the bandits on the hilltop he did not want to think. They still didn't seem real—just movies that had never actually happened. For now, at least, he wanted to keep them that way. Perhaps later, when he got home, he could talk about them.

He heard Benton stir, and turned on his side. Jack smiled sleepily. "Did you have a good night, Ken? I waked a couple of times and felt as though a horse was lying on my chest. I couldn't breathe until I sat up."

"I was all right," Ken said. "Slept like a log. But what about this rain? Think we can hunt?"

"Not unless it stops. We're pretty far up in the sky, really in the clouds. I'll bet there is sun down in the valley."

By the time they were dressed, Wu brought in breakfast. Latunga was right behind him.

"What about it?" Benton asked the Moso.

"Can do. Pretty soon the rain will stop. We'll surely find goral on that cliff above the meadow."

"Want to have a go at it, Ken? You'll get wet."

"Yes, but what will you do?"

"Don't worry about me. I'll set fifty or sixty traps. This mountain ought to be alive with small mammals. I'll bet my shirt most of them will be new species, too, for no one has worked anywhere near here. You don't know how exciting it is to trap the small stuff. I'll start you at it tomorrow."

The men stepped outside the tent. Latunga pointed to a ragged cliff above them. "I'll send the other two hunters with the dogs behind that rocky shoulder, and we'll go up this side. If a goral is there it'll surely run around toward us. Let's go."

By the time they had worked through the dripping forest onto an open hillside the rain had ceased, but dense clouds drifted in and out among the peaks. In less than half an hour the thin wail of yelping hounds floated out of the fog. Latunga listened intently, then made signs for Ken to hurry. The Moso scrambled, catlike, up the steep slope. Ken tried to follow, but in a few seconds his pounding heart stopped him cold. No good, he thought. I couldn't shoot. Have to rest.

Sitting on a rock, he gasped for breath. Suddenly the dogs swept around the cliff near the summit. Just in front of them a bounding gray form showed like a wraith for a moment; then the mist closed in, and Ken lost both hounds and quarry until a blessed gust of wind drifted the fog away. There stood the goral on a narrow shelf with its back to the rock wall, facing the pack. Big Red dashed in, but with a quick lunge and up-thrust of its head the beast caught the dog on its curved horns and tossed him over the cliff. Big Red whirled in the air, spread out like a red rag, and dropped into a snowdrift two hundred feet beneath the ledge. Latunga screamed and gesticulated wildly, imploring Ken to hurry.

"No use," Ken panted. "I'll try it from here." The Moso

realized Ken was going to shoot from where he was. It seemed madness, but he watched Ken settle into a hollow and poke his rifle across a rock.

Three hundred yards at least, Ken thought. But it's my only hope.

He could barely see the gray form through the rear peep sight. As he touched the trigger a white dog dashed in, nipping at the goral's throat. Just in time, Ken threw up the rifle, and the bullet splashed loose stones above the animal. The goral lashed out viciously, and the hound backed off. Ken fired again. The beast gave a convulsive leap, plunging off the ledge into the snowdrift beside the red dog.

Latunga stared incredulously and then seemed to go completely mad. He hugged Ken, pounded him on the back, and kowtowed, touching his forehead to the ground. Grabbing the rifle, he rubbed it against his face and cradled it in his arms, mumbling words that must have been a prayer. A moment later he scrambled down the canyon, leaping from rock to rock and swinging from one bush to another like a monkey in the treetops.

Ken followed at a snail's pace. When he arrived Latunga was kneeling beside Big Red, tears streaming from his eyes. The hound had a long gash in the flesh of his breast, from which blood oozed in a slow stream. He was alive, and when Ken bandaged the wound with his handkerchief he tried to lick the boy's hands. The Moso shouted to the hunters picking their way down the almost vertical cliff, telling them to bring the goral. Then, as tenderly as a mother, he took the hurt dog in his arms and started back to camp.

Benton had just arrived from a reconnaissance of the meadow. Ken rapidly sketched what had happened. Jack got his surgical kit and with a few stitches sewed the edges of the wound together. The dog lay quietly with his eyes fixed on Latunga's face. The pupils dilated with pain, but not once did the animal whine or stir. Benton patted Latunga's shoulder. "Don't worry. Big Red will be all right in a few days. He is weak now from loss of blood. It is only a deep flesh wound."

The Moso's face broke into a smile. "Had it not been for the young master and his wonderful gun, other dogs would have been killed. Never did I dream there could be such a gun. I thought he was crazy to shoot. It was so far I could hardly see the goral, but he kneeled behind a rock, pointed the gun, and *pouf*, the animal was dead."

"Must have been a pretty good shot, Ken," Benton said. "Glad you were the one to take it. I'd probably have knocked over half the dogs before I got the beast. Here it comes. Let's have a look."

They examined it curiously.

"Ken, do you know to what sub-family the gorals belong?"

"Yes, the *Rupicaprinæ*. Also it has the serows and the takin, which is more closely allied to the musk ox. They're entirely Asiatic. But the chamois of Europe and the Rocky Mountain goat of America are members too. They migrated from Asia a long time ago. Is that right?"

"Absolutely, so far. Why are the *Rupicaprinæ* called 'goat antelopes'?"

"Because they combine characters of both goats and antelopes. They hold a sort of intermediate position between the two."

Benton grinned. "You've passed a hundred per cent. You seem to know my book *The Mammals of Asia* pretty well."

"I ought to. I've studied it enough."

The goral was buff-gray in color and looked much like a chamois. The sharp six-inch horns were definitely dangerous.

One of them still showed the blood of Big Red on its tip. Ken's bullet had entered just behind the left foreleg and emerged at the base of the neck on the other side. He showed the Mosos the tiny cartridge, and they could only shake their heads in wonder. This was beyond their understanding.

When Benton prepared to skin the animal, Latunga asked to take charge before the Americans touched the body. Jack knew it was their ritual for the God of the Hunt. All primitive natives have something of the sort. He wondered what this would be. One of the men cut a leafy branch to make a bed for the dead goral. While chanting a prayer, Latunga carefully opened the body, removed the heart, and sliced off the tip. After wrapping it in several layers of green leaves, he placed the package in the crotch of a tree, and the three Mosos kowtowed, touching their foreheads to the ground. Latunga motioned to Ken to do the same. Then Latunga divided the remainder of the heart in four parts and offered one to Ken. The natives ate their bits with relish.

"You've got to go through with it," Jack muttered. Ken swallowed his portion in one gulp.

"Now we'll have good hunting all the days we are here," said Latunga.

Ken laughed. "Never did I dream I'd eat raw heart! Wonder what Mother would say? Probably she'd be horrified, but Dad would think it wonderful."

"You'll have to do worse things than that before you're through in China. If you hadn't eaten that piece of heart and kowtowed, the Mosos would believe you had insulted their God of the Hunt and that he'd make you miss the next animal you shot at. Now they'll work like everything for you. Let's skin this goral."

After luncheon Jack picked up a bag of wooden traps.

"You're about to have your first lesson in trapping. We'll set a line in the woods and then go into the meadow. The animals will be different in each place."

Just beyond the edge of the forest Benton stopped at a huge fallen tree. Tiny pathways in the soft earth margined the rotting trunk. "These are runways, Ken, the village streets of woodmice, shrews, and other small things. They always follow the same path along a log, so we'll set two or three traps on each side and a couple in the roots." Peanut butter was the bait, and a bit of cotton on a bush was to mark each trap. Jack gave the bag to Ken. "Now it's up to you. I'll stand on the sideline and keep you straight." Ken selected spots beneath roots and moss at the foot of trees and at the entrances to little holes if they looked as though they had been recently used.

The meadow was much simpler. Under the long grass an intricate pattern of tiny tunnels ran in every direction. "Those are made by voles, *Microtus*," Jack said. "You saw dozens of them, Ken, in my collections, but you didn't know how I got them. Now you'll find out. None of the lowland forms would be able to live at this altitude, and these will certainly be a new species. I'll name it for you—*Microtus lewisi*. For all the rest of your life, and till the end of time, a little brown meadow mouse will be running about on the Snow Mountain, tagged with your name. Aren't you thrilled?"

Ken laughed. "Of course. It's like getting a medal. But the mouse won't know it, and Latunga won't, if he ever sees one."

"That's true, but all the scientific world will know. And they'll know too that Ken Lewis trapped the first one on the Snow Mountain. Darned few white men have even seen the Snow Mountain, and none have been where you and I stand right now. That's a distinction; in a way it is a record of your travels, and you'll appreciate it when you are older."

"Do you have a lot of things named after you, Jack?"

"Sure. Every collector has. Snakes and lizards, mammals, birds, and a lot of insects, particularly ants. I have a great friend, Professor William Morton Wheeler. He was Curator of Entomology at the American Museum for many years, and then he went to Harvard University. He is the greatest authority on ants in the world. Wherever I go, I collect ants for him. He has named a dozen new species for me, but never two in the same place. It's a sort of game with us. When I die, if someone wants to plot my wanderings, he can look up the ants named *bentoni*—and, of course, the other things too. It would be a pretty accurate chart of my travels as a naturalist."

"I never thought of it that way," Ken said. "Gosh, I hope this little mouse is new! I'd really like him as my namesake."

That evening a brilliant moon shone with a soft white light, turning the Snow Mountain peak to dazzling silver and opening mysterious vistas in the forest wall. After dinner Jack announced, "We'll go out and run the traps. There's a double chance that way. Those that are full now perhaps will catch another specimen before morning."

With flashlights and a shotgun the men picked their way among the trees until the first bits of cotton showed on twigs above a fallen log. In one trap a tiny shrew struggled, caught by the tail as it was running across the trap; another held a white-footed mouse, and a third a small rat with sharp spines mixed in the fur. The traps in the old root had been sprung but were empty. Jack dropped the specimens in the pocket of his hunting coat and reset the traps. Ken whispered, "Gee, this is fun. It's like opening Christmas packages. I can hardly wait to see the others."

Deep in the woods, where a dozen traps nestled in runways

under thick moss, they snapped off the lights and sat down on a log. Quiet dropped over the forest like a falling curtain—complete, absolute silence! Then, slowly, the night creatures resumed their way of life. Almost beside them tiny feet scurried in the dry leaves. A fox answered the hoarse bark of a muntjac across the canyon. Even the treetops seemed alive. Dead twigs dropped to the ground, and soft-winged owls showed black against openings in the branches. Just beyond a fallen log two greenish spots of light suddenly appeared. Ken touched Jack's arm and pointed. "What is it?" he breathed, his lips close to Benton's ear.

"Don't know. Shoot."

A streak of flame ripped through the darkness, and echoes beat against the mountain walls, piling back upon themselves in waves of sound. Ken reloaded quickly and moved toward the log. His flashlight showed a dark animal the size of a small dog, lying on the ground. "It's a porcupine," Jack said, "and a buster too. Look at those quills—must be a foot long. Wouldn't they ruin a pack of hounds! Once they get into flesh they keep going deeper and deeper as the muscles work, and you can't pull them out. It's a beautiful specimen. I'll give you the job of skinning it tomorrow."

"Don't know how I can skin a thing like that! Guess I'll have to use gloves."

"No you won't. It's easy enough if you work in the direction that the quills lie. It's only when the animal is annoyed that they stand out straight."

"Can they actually throw them like darts? I've heard that our American porcupines do."

"No, of course not. That story got started because a porc can switch his tail about like lightning, and the quills come out at the slightest touch. You'll see when you skin this fellow. If you don't work very gently most of the quills will be on the table. Let's run the rest of the trap-line."

As they emerged from the forest Latunga stumbled toward them, carrying a pine torch. His face broke into a delighted grin when he saw the porcupine. "Very good to eat. Very good. Better than pig. Perhaps you will give Latunga some."

Benton laughed. "You can have the whole thing after we get the skin off. We'll stick to goral meat."

In the tent they spread their specimens on the folding table. Shrews of three species, two moles, woodmice, and four spiny rats. Jack looked at them with great satisfaction. "A fine haul. Probably we'll have twice as many by morning. Then there'll be a job to get their skins off. This place will be an absolute gold mine, for I'm willing to bet every one of these represents a species new to science. Couldn't be otherwise in this isolated locality and at this altitude. Gosh, Ken, we'll have fun when we get back to the museum and study these collections. It's almost as exciting as doing the field work.

"In the morning you run the traps while I start to make up these skins. Then I suggest that you go out with Latunga and see if you can get a serow. When you come back you can help me on whatever remains. Is that okay with you?"

"Sure is, but don't you want to hunt too? You're giving me all the fun."

"No I'm not. I'll get a great kick out of working on these small things and making provisional identification. Moreover, you're a better shot than I am, and you can travel the mountain better than I can. You'll find it will be hard work to stick with the Mosos in this thin air. I'm ten years older than you are, and, believe it or not, that makes a difference. Let's turn in."

IX. Terror in the Forest

NEITHER Jack Benton nor Ken Lewis suspected that visiting a line of small mammal traps less than a half-mile from camp would result in near tragedy. But in that beautiful sunlit morning at the Snow Mountain, Ken came very close to death. Afterward for many nights, if he got up in the dark and his feet touched something soft and yielding, he leaped like a frightened stag. Never in his life had he been so utterly terrified.

It began very simply. After breakfast he slung two canvas bags over his shoulders and started across the meadow. Benton looked up from the table where he was skinning mice and called, "Ken, you haven't got a gun."

"No. You told me to collect all the traps, and it would be a nuisance to carry. I won't need it."

"Probably not, but I've always made it a rule not to leave camp without a rifle or pistol. Better put on your thirty-eight."

Ken returned to the tent and strapped the Colt revolver about his waist.

"Another thing, Ken. If you are ever in trouble and need help, fire three shots quickly, one after the other. Don't know why I didn't tell you before. I've used that signal ever since I've been in the field, and it means 'come at once' to whoever hears it."

"All right, I'll remember."

Just within the edge of the trees Ken picked up the line of cotton and followed it deep into the forest. His pockets were full of little beasts, and the bags bulged with traps. At the edge of an open glade where the sun lay in pools of brilliant gold, he sat down on a log and lighted his pipe. The blue smoke curled over his head, mingling with the scent of spruce trees and crushed ferns. Through the branches the white spire of the mountain's central peak cut into the sky. He appraised it speculatively. Wonder if Jack will climb that before we leave. We could go up along the west ridge. Of course the snow might be tough, and twenty thousand feet is getting pretty well up in the air. He probably won't do it. After all, mountain-climbing isn't our job. Guess I'd better move if I'm going out with Latunga.

He knocked the ashes from his pipe, picked up his bags, and plunged into the mass of waist-high ferns toward bits of cotton showing on the dead branches of a fallen spruce. In the deep hollow under the roots, he remembered, Jack had set five mousetraps. It was a big tree, overlaid with thick moss. Ken swung one leg, then the other, across the trunk, and slipped down into the depression. His feet struck something soft and alive, something that sent prickles of fear up his spine into the roots of his scalp. Before he could move, a mountainous, hairy mass heaved upward, and a great clawed hand reached for his neck. Instinctively he ducked, but the hand struck his shoulder. The blow ripped off the trap bags, tore away his shirt, and pitched him headlong into the underbrush. He lay quiet, paralyzed with terror. He realized that he had dropped onto a bear, asleep in the hole beneath the tree root.

The beast was standing erect, tearing madly at one of the canvas bags, scattering traps in every direction. Ken twisted on his side and pulled his revolver from its holster. The movement caught the bear's eye. With a choking roar it threw itself on Ken's body. He had a momentary picture of foam-flecked teeth and two bloodshot eyes staring into his. Jamming the pistol against the hairy neck, he pressed the trigger. At the muffled explosion the bear quivered and sank down, stretched across his breast like a sleeping dog.

For a time Ken lay still, too frightened to move; then he drew himself from under the heavy black body. He tried to stand, but his knees buckled under him and he collapsed beside the bear. Finally he crawled to the fallen tree and sat with his back against the trunk. One thought came clear in his mind. Jack had said when he left the tent, "If you're in trouble, shoot three times."

The echoes of Ken's shots had hardly died away when an answer came from camp. Minutes later shouts sounded in the forest. He tried to call, but his voice died in his throat and he fired the revolver again. Suddenly Latunga burst through the underbrush and leaped over the tree. In one horrified glance he saw the dead bear, and Ken half lying against the log, covered with blood. The Moso cupped his hands and gave a long halloo.

The boy managed to get to his feet when Benton arrived, gasping for breath. "Ken—are you—all right?"

"I guess so. I stepped on a bear. It's over there—dead."

Jack stripped off what remained of Ken's shirt. Blood oozed slowly from a long furrow in his shoulder, and an ugly bruise was already beginning to swell. After a careful examination he stood up in relief. "Thank God, it's only a flesh wound. You'll be all right soon. What happened?"

Ken sat down on the log. "Can you get me my pipe? It's in my left pants pocket. I'm feeling fine now, only my shoulder burns like fire, and it's stiff. Gee, I'm glad you're here."

Latunga squatted in front of them while Ken told his story. Benton translated rapidly. The Moso nodded. "It was the God of the Hunt. He saved your life." Then they looked at the bear. The .38-caliber slug had smashed the neck vertebrae to pulp and cut the spinal cord at the base of the skull. "If you'd had an hour to pick a vital spot you couldn't have done better, Ken. That's about the only place where a revolver bullet would have killed the beast before it chewed you up."

"I can't take any credit for it. I just stuck the gun under the bear's chin and pulled the trigger. I didn't think; there wasn't time. Gosh, that face looking into mine! It was horrible!"

"You certainly are lucky. Imagine stepping on a bear in the woods and coming out alive! Never heard of anything like it. Might not happen again in a hundred years! Let's go back to camp. I want to put some antiseptic on that shoulder. Probably there'll be no infection, but we can't take chances. Latunga will get the other hunters and bring in the bear."

Wu and the cook stood anxiously about the table while Benton washed Ken's shoulder with potassium permanganate. A livid furrow ran from neck to waist across the back. Benton dried the wound, covered it with soothing ointment, and bandaged it. "It's a good thing you ducked when he swung that haymaker at you, Ken. If a claw had gone in at the base of your neck you'd have been a dead chicken."

"Will it leave a scar?"

Benton's eyes twinkled. "Yes, a beautiful scar. When you go bathing all the girls will gasp and get big-eyed at your battle with the bear."

"I—I didn't mean that," Ken stammered. Nevertheless, he was thinking of Carol Whitehouse.

Jack smiled. "You needn't get upset. You have a right to be proud of it. I wish I had one like it. Mighty few men in the world have fought hand to hand with a raging bear and come out alive. It was pure, unadulterated guts and straight thinking that brought you through. No medal you'll ever get will mean what this scar does."

"I was so scared I thought I'd die. The fight with the bandits was nothing like this. Then I knew what would probably happen and was prepared, but when I landed on that bear it seemed like a horrible nightmare."

"Well, the skin belongs to you. That is one specimen that won't go to the museum. Here it comes."

The Mosos were staggering under the weight of the carcass, which swung on a carrying pole between them. They dropped it beside the fire with relief.

"Three hundred pounds at least," Latunga said. "Fat as a pig."

The animal was coal-black except for the brown muzzle and

a white V-shaped mark on the breast. Latunga prepared for the sacrificial ceremony to the God of the Hunt. Ken did his kowtow and ate his bit of heart with no reluctance. Whatever god there was who lived in the forest had been pretty good to him!

In spite of Ken's protests, Benton insisted that he lie down for a rest. In two minutes he was lost in a sleep of utter exhaustion. It was past noon before he waked. He was stiff, and his shoulder burned unmercifully, but otherwise he felt well.

Benton sat at the table, skinning mice. "Can I help?" Ken asked.

"Yes, this is going to be your job for the next few days until your shoulder heals. I'll go out with Latunga tomorrow and try for a serow. We've got forty-five specimens to prepare, and you can help me set another line of traps. I told you this place would be a gold mine for small stuff, and it surely is. We have eight species of shrews already, and your meadow mouse is certainly new. It will be *Microtus lewisi* without a doubt."

Ken began work. Each little animal was numbered and measured—total length, tail, and hind foot. Then the skin was stripped off, dusted with arsenic, and stuffed lightly with cotton. A wire was run down the tail. The skull was numbered, like the skin. Ken had learned to "make up" small mammal skins, but he watched Jack with envy. "You've done five in thirty minutes, and I've only finished two. What's the matter with me?"

"Nothing. Nothing at all. It's only practice. I've been doing this continually for more than ten years. You've got good hands, and by the end of the season you'll equal me. It's only a matter of making every motion count. I enjoy it, for this is what makes an expedition worth while. Most of the big mammals in the world have already been discovered and named, but thousands of small beasts are still unknown, and they show us the laws of nature. When we study this collection, back in New York, you will see how the flora, climate and altitude, and geographical separation by rivers and mountains influence the formation of species. Collection in the field is exciting and interesting, but its importance lies in telling the scientific world what new facts the specimens show."

By four o'clock all the skins were pinned neatly in wooden trays that fitted one on top of another in the collecting trunks. Jack stood up and stretched. "Let's put out another line of traps and have an early night. I'll try for a serow with La-tunga in the morning. He says we'll surely find one in the thick spruce forest below where you shot the goral."

"I suppose I won't feel like going out tomorrow, but I'd like to shoot a serow," Ken said. "From the skins we saw in the market I'd guess they are three times as big as a goral."

"Yes, and three times as savage. They're really bad customers, Latunga says. Almost every one kills a dog or two, and the natives aren't keen about hunting them."

Ken did not sleep well. His shoulder hurt, and a vivid nightmare of menacing claws and a revolver that wouldn't shoot chased itself through his dreams. He awoke dripping with sweat. After pulling on his shirt and trousers, he stepped outside the tent. The fire showed only as a heap of glowing coals, but he tossed on split pine sticks and the flames leaped up, throwing weird shadows against the blackness of the forest. Lighting his pipe, he sat down on a log, where the heat waves wrapped themselves about his body.

A mound just beyond the fire moved, and Latunga sat up. He had made a nest for himself in a pile of leaves outside the tent door. The Moso rubbed his eyes and came over to sit on the log. Ken offered him his tobacco pouch. The two smoked quietly in a companionship that had no need for words. Gradually Ken felt his tense nerves relax, and a delicious drowsiness envelop his senses. Smiling at Latunga, he opened the tent flaps and slipped into the soft fur of his sleeping bag.

X. Crossbow and Poisoned Arrows

IN THE morning Benton left with the hunters shortly after
daylight. After climbing slowly through a bank of cloud so
thick that men and dogs seemed like gray ghosts, they emerged
on the edge of a canyon where the sun lay bright and warm.
Benton sat down while the hounds scattered among the rocks.
Suddenly one yelped on a ridge above them, and the rest of
the pack dashed up the mountainside. In a few moments they
all gave tongue. "Goral," Latunga said, "coming this way."

Just then the thick mass of cloud began to drift upward in
a long, thin finger out of the canyon. It came swiftly, and

closer and closer sounded the voices of the hounds. Jack was trembling with impatience and swearing softly as the gray vapors streamed from the gorge, wrapping the men in an impenetrable blanket. A moment later they heard the goral leaping down the cliff not a dozen yards away. Benton stood with the rifle useless in his hands, listening to each hoofbeat and the stones that the flying feet sent rattling into the chasm. Then the dogs came past, their music growing fainter and fainter in the smothering fog.

Ten minutes later a puff of wind sucked the cloud back into the ravine as rapidly as it had come. Above them shone a sky as clear and blue as a tropic sea. The hunters picked their way slowly down the steep hillside and reached the edge of the spruce forest. The cries of the hounds became louder and more insistent. Suddenly they rose in a chorus of frenzied yelps.

Latunga plunged into the woods, calling over his shoulder, "Serow. They've got a serow."

Even though their path was downhill, the air at thirteen thousand feet was too thin for Jack. His heart pounded, and he gasped for breath. The natives were beyond sight in a moment, but he could hear them crashing through the underbrush far below.

At last he reached the edge of a deep and narrow ravine. On the opposite side a cutback in the rock wall formed a wide shelf. Half crouched in a corner was a great black animal with donkey-like ears. Head lowered, it snorted defiance at the snarling pack. A dog rushed in. The serow twisted and, with a vicious upthrust of its dagger-like horns, ripped the hound wide open. Another dog leaped for the serow's throat. The animal reared backward, striking out with its front feet. The dog sprang wide of its quarry, was caught in mid-air and sent whirling over and over into the depths of the ravine. It looked

CROSSBOW AND POISONED ARROWS 101

as though half the pack would be killed, but the dancing beasts never gave Benton a chance to shoot. Time after time he sighted at the black body but did not dare press the trigger.

Then, in an overhanging tree above and to the left, he saw a flurry of leaves. A man climbed out on a branch like a great ape, hung suspended by one hand, and dropped to the ledge right among the dogs. It was Latunga.

Jack was horrified. If the serow dashed forward only a few feet, the Moso was a dead man. He would either be speared by the rapier-sharp horns or be knocked over the brink onto the rocks a hundred feet below.

When Latunga appeared so suddenly the serow snorted, pressed back against the cliff, and eyed him malevolently. At any second it might charge. But the little Moso seemed completely unconcerned. Deliberately he pulled the crossbow off his back and strung it. He drew the bear's-paw quiver around in front of his body, selected an arrow, rejected it, and took another. He examined the tip critically, seemed satisfied, and fitted it to the string. Then he sighted quickly. The sharp twang of the crossbow sounded even above the clamor of the dogs.

The serow surged up and forward almost onto the Moso. Benton thought it would plunge off the shelf, but at the very edge it shuddered and sank down on its belly, the white-maned neck between its forelegs. Latunga had said the poison acted in about the time it took to light a pipe. This was quicker than that. Benton found out why afterward. The arrow was embedded in the heart!

Jack worked slowly around the head of the ravine and joined the hunters. He was thrilled at what Latunga had done, but the Moso took it as a matter of course—nothing out of the usual. He had seen that Benton couldn't shoot, and a man had to save his dogs! He didn't know where he would find two others to replace those that had been killed. The best ones always went first. They were the most venturesome.

"Why didn't you shoot from the tree?" Jack asked.

Latunga smiled. "There would have been no excitement in that," he said, "and I might have hit a hound."

The serow would weigh about three hundred pounds—many times larger than a goral. He was brownish-black with rusty-red lower legs and a whitish mane. The right horn measured nine and three-quarters inches long and five and three-quarters inches in circumference at the base. The body was badly scarred from fighting. Because of the long, melancholy-looking face and the big ears, the Chinese call the serow the "wild donkey." Latunga said that serows liked to sleep under overhanging rocks and on the steep shelves of ravines. They seldom came out into the open, but fed on leaves and grass while in the thickest cover. It would be almost impossible to kill them without the aid of dogs or beaters.

After Jack had prepared the skin, skull, and legbones of the serow, the two hunters packed the specimens on their backs and started for camp. Latunga and Benton climbed out of the forest with the hounds in front. At the edge of the meadow the pack gave tongue. Latunga listened for a moment and motioned Jack to stop. He ran fifty yards to the left and sank down in the grass beside a granite boulder. From over a hogback a goral bounced as though it were on rubber feet and made straight for Latunga's rock. As it passed, the crossbow twanged. The animal staggered but kept running. It had almost reached Jack, and his rifle sights were on its nose, when it crumpled like a piece of wet paper. The poisoned arrow was embedded nearly to the hilt in the animal's side. Latunga was delighted. He threw his arms about Benton, pounded him on the back, and held the crossbow at arm's length in the air. He had good reason to be proud. Twice within two hours he had shown that it could be as effective as a high-powered rifle.

Latunga tied the forelegs of the goral loosely together and slipped his head between them. The hind legs fitted about his waist. The animal made a neat package that rode well on his back. It weighed sixty pounds, but the little Moso walked off with his load as though it had been a bundle of feathers. The altitude seemed to make no difference to him, but Jack had difficulty in keeping pace.

At camp, Ken saw them as they emerged from the forest, and ran halfway across the meadow. The hunters with the serow had already arrived, and he had been working on the skin. Bits of flesh and fat had to be removed before it could be salted.

When they reached the tent he showed Jack fifteen small mammal skins neatly pinned in the trays. "That's my morning's work," he said proudly. "There are ten more, but I thought you would rather have me get the serow skin ready for salting. Isn't it an extraordinary-looking animal! Not much like a goral, except for the horns. But from the skulls I can see how they are related. Where did you kill it?"

Over a cup of tea Jack told him the story. Ken was fascinated. "What a wonderful little guy Latunga is. I've never seen anybody like him. Already I'm awfully fond of him. He is so sympathetic and understanding, and so gentle, but there's nothing he can't do. I hope he'll stay with us."

"I do too. He's the best native hunter I've ever had. These Mosos are really fine people. According to Major Davies' book, they were originally an independent race and ruled a large part of northern Yunnan. Lichiang was their capital. Davies says that even now they outnumber all the other aborigines in this region. Their customs are semi-Tibetan."

"By the way, Jack, the cook gave me some of Latunga's buttered tea and *tsampa* for luncheon. He made it last night. Did you ever taste buttered tea?"

"No. Of course it's what the Tibetans live on almost entirely. Was it good?"

"I liked it. Cook said Latunga made it by churning butter into hot tea until they were well mixed. Then he thickened it with the parched barley they call *tsampa*. You ought to try some."

"I will. The natives here certainly live better than in any other part of China that I've seen. You won't get fresh milk or butter and such wonderful fruit and vegetables anywhere else. Even the poorest people look well fed. Of course, it is due to the summer rain and the warm winter. It gives a long growing season. I forgot to ask what you caught in the traps this morning? Anything new?"

"Yes, two species of shrews we've not had before, and a mole. There are half a dozen small rats and a number of white-footed mice. I suppose they are *Apodemus*."

"Probably. If three-quarters of the small mammals aren't species new to science, I'll be surprised."

Suddenly, from well away in the forest, came the sharp yelp of a hound. Latunga ran out from the cook tent.

"That's Big Red. He went off by himself just after we came in. He's driving something this way. Better get your gun."

Ken ran into the tent and grabbed his Mannlicher rifle. Just as he emerged a yellow-red animal twice the size of a fox burst from the edge of the woods. In long leaps it dashed across the meadow, a hundred yards from the tents. Ken dropped to one knee and fired just as the little beast rose into the air. It turned a complete somersault. Everyone in camp cheered. Latunga hugged the boy.

Jack pounded him on the back. "By golly, that was a wonderful shot! I'll never forget it. I'd give my shirt if I could shoot as well as you do."

Ken glowed with happiness. "I sure do like to shoot," he said.

One of the Mosos brought in the animal. It was a muntjac, the beautiful little deer of South China. Its antlers were only three inches long and rose from an elongated, skin-covered pedicel of bone, instead of from the base of the skull as in all other deer. On each side of the upper jaw a slender, knife-sharp tusk projected for two inches below the lip.

"Do you remember, Ken, that we saw one of these little chaps while we were hunting tiger in Fukien? This is a larger species, but I'll bet he'll be just as good eating. We'll let him hang for a couple of days, and then you'll have the tenderest, sweetest meat you ever tasted. Now I want to see you skin him. You'll have to 'case' it, for it might be mounted."

Ken laid the animal on its back and made a cut from the middle of the breast to the root of the tail; then he worked the skin away from the body with a pusher and the haft of his knife. By cutting the back side of each foot for a few inches at the hock and disjointing the bone, the leg could be slipped out, leaving the skin intact. The only other incision was on the back of the head, to remove the skull.

"Carl Akeley, the famous artist-taxidermist, was the one who first used that method of skinning short-haired mammals," Benton said. "He taught me himself. When the animal is mounted there are no seams to show. Now salt the skin and roll it up. Be sure to push a lot of salt down the legs and around the hoofs."

After dinner, while they were sitting about the campfire, Ken asked, "What's the program for tomorrow?"

"How do you feel? Want to go out with the Mosos?"

"Yes, I'd like to. I'm fine. My shoulder is sore and a little stiff, but that's all. Probably in the morning I'll hardly feel it. Big Red seems to be all right too."

"I want to get a group of goral for the North Asiatic Hall in the museum. We have two good bucks. Now we need a female and a couple of young. Of course we must have more serow too. Latunga will be happy to take you out. He likes me, but you're his protégé. You'll learn a lot from him."

"I know it. Wish I could speak more Chinese. We understand each other well enough, but I can't exchange thoughts with him. I suppose that someday I'll be able to speak Chinese as well as you do, but it's a tough language."

"You'll learn it eventually if you stay here. Remember I've had a long time in China. Let's turn in. You'll want to leave at daylight."

Ken reached camp late the next afternoon with three goral. One was a female and the other two yearling bucks.

Benton was delighted. "These are exactly what we needed for the group. We'll give the hounds a rest tomorrow and get the accessory material. I know just the spot for the group. It's less than a mile from here."

The place he had selected was an almost perpendicular rock-wall broken into ledges, pinnacles, and deep cracks. Latunga agreed that it was a typical goral cliff. Jack took a dozen photographs to aid the museum artists in reproducing the background. Then he collected samples of the rock and bits of moss and leaves that could be dried or preserved in formalin. Ken found it interesting work, and even Latunga caught the excitement, although he could not understand what it was all about.

For two weeks the expedition remained at the camp in the meadow on the Snow Mountain. Benton stuck pretty closely to the trapping of small mammals, while Ken went out almost every day with the Mosos. He killed three serows, four or five more gorals, and another bear. Most interesting scientifically was a crested muntjac (*Elaphodus*). The animal was the size of a greyhound and dark bluish-slate in color. Latunga said that in all his years of hunting he had seen not more than five or six. Jack was delighted. "These," he said, "are as scarce as hens' teeth in collections. I've only seen one skin in the British Museum. There are none in America."

The night before breaking camp Benton and Latunga sat long before the fire, talking. Until then Jack had not asked the Moso if he would go with them into the northern mountains for the snow leopard. With a smile Latunga confessed that this had been a test trip. Hunting and living in the forest and seeing new country were his greatest joys in life. His friends were happy to remain in the village with their wives and children. But he could not. Seldom did he take anyone with him. He preferred to be alone. The wild creatures, the great trees, and the mountains were company enough. They were the companions he loved most.

"Until you spoke to me in the market place at Lichiang," he said, "I had never seen a man like you. It wasn't your skin color and dress that surprised me, so much as your blue eyes. You were like a being from another world. Then, at the temple, I saw your guns and traps and the skins of mice and rats and small beasts all pinned out in trays. That made me very curious.

What kind of man would catch little animals? You told me you spent your whole life doing that! Never had I heard of such a thing. Certainly it would be interesting to find out more about you and see if I could be happy with you in the mountains. I have been happy. I will go with you wherever you wish."

Latunga told his thoughts in simple Chinese words. He did not try to analyze why he was not like other men, who stayed at home, or why he was happy only in the wilderness and must always search for new country. But Benton knew why. Latunga was a born explorer, just as Jack was, and just as Ken Lewis was. The special breed is as old as the human race. Some member of the earliest tribe felt the inborn urge to see what lay beyond the horizon's rim. He found new hunting grounds and led his people to other valleys. Thus the earth today is known to its uttermost limits.

In some ways Latunga was the most primitive human being Jack had ever known. To physical comfort he seemed completely indifferent. He slept in the open and seldom twice in the same place. Sometimes he curled up on the lee side of a boulder if the wind was blowing. Next night his bed might be at the root of a larch tree. Often it was in a pile of leaves. His only covering was his brown felt cape. He laughed when Benton offered him a fur sleeping bag, saying that in it he would suffocate.

Jack asked why he would not sleep in the cook tent. "I like to feel the night wind on my face," Latunga said, "and to look up at the stars. And when all is quiet the small creatures begin to move about. Then I am a part of the forest as one can never be in the daylight. It is good to sleep in the open."

XI. The Great Gorge of the Yangtze River

OCTOBER had slipped into November when the expedition shifted camp to the "White Water" on the other side of the Snow Mountain. After crossing the *gangheisa*, or "dry sea," a great grassy plain, they followed a trail into the forest and down the bottom of a deep canyon. The water of a mountain stream spread itself in a thin green veil over a bed of pure white stones.

The tents were pitched on a broad terrace beside the brook at the edge of a spruce forest. Above them towered the highest peak of the mountain, with a glacier nestling in a basin near the summit. Snow-covered slopes extended in a glorious shining crescent about the camp. The moon was full. As they sat at dinner before the fire, the ragged peaks turned crimson in the afterglow of the sun, and changed to purest silver at the touch of the moonlight. Ken thought he had never seen anything so beautiful.

While they were at breakfast the first morning, a bird call sounded from a spruce tree close to camp. "That's a pheasant," Benton said. "I wonder which one it is! I know there are several forest-living species in this region. See if you can get it."

Ken ducked through the tent door for his shotgun and moved silently into the woods. Jack watched him slip from tree to tree, like an Indian, cleverly stalking the spruce so that the bird must fly out into the open.

That boy is a born hunter, he thought. No one taught him that. It's as natural to him as breathing.

Suddenly, from the lower branches of the tree, a rainbow flashed across the terrace. As the gun roared, the bird dropped to the ground. Ken picked it up by one leg. "Jack, what a gorgeous thing! Look at that tail, and that white and green ruff! It's a pheasant, of course, but which one?"

"Lady Amherst. It was named for the Countess of Amherst. She was one of the loveliest women in England. When the first pair of these birds were brought alive to London, they were presented to her and given her name. She ought to have been complimented."

"We can't just strip off the feathers and eat it. It's too beautiful."

"You're dead right. We'll make it up for the collection. You'll get your first lesson in bird-skinning right now."

Ken watched while Benton plugged the pheasant's throat with cotton. "That," he said, "is to keep blood or juices from getting on the feathers." Then he made an incision from the middle of the breast to the root of the tail, and worked the skin off the body with his fingers. Cornmeal was continually dusted on the exposed flesh to absorb moisture or blood. After snipping off the legs at the knee joints, and the root of the tail, he turned the skin inside out, and cut off the neck at the base of the skull. Then he held up the skin by the bill, dusted the flesh side with arsenic, and filled it with cotton. A few stitches closed the incision. The whole procedure had not consumed more than twelve minutes.

For a week the men camped at the White Water. Big game was not abundant, but Ken and the Mosos killed a fine serow and a young goral. Benton was disappointed that his traps yielded few species of small mammals new to their collections.

"It's time we moved farther north," he said to Ken. "I want to go across the great bend of the Yangtze. The river ought to act as a distribution barrier to most of the small mammals. I imagine we'll get a different fauna on the other side."

Two days later they stood on the summit of a pine-covered ridge, looking at a sight that made them gasp. Far below, the mighty Yangtze, flowing southward from its birthplace in the Tibetan steppes, had found the great Snow Mountain range barring its path. Thrust aside, it doubled back upon itself, along the barrier's base, seeking a passage through the wall of rock. Far to the north it bit hungrily into the mountainside again, broke through, and swung southward in a gorge almost a mile deep—a gorge that seems to have been cut sharp and clean with a giant's knife. In places the rocks show delicate tints of yellow, red, blue, and purple; at others the sides fall away in sheer drops of hundreds of feet to the green torrent rushing to the sea two thousand miles away.

"It's almost as wonderful as the Grand Canyon of the

Colorado," Benton said. "Just think—probably not a dozen white men have ever seen this place. We're pretty fortunate."

"We surely are. I've never been to the Grand Canyon, but it seems as though nothing could be more impressive than this. How will we ever get across the river?"

"Latunga says this trail leads to a village called Taku. There's a break in the canyon there, and the natives have a ferry. The boat is only big enough to carry two mules at a time. He says the current is very strong and that it will take all day to get our caravan across."

Latunga was right. By nightfall only twelve of the twenty-six mules were over the river. The expedition made camp in one of a dozen caverns that honeycombed the rock wall. Some were occupied by natives; others seemed to have been abandoned. A central shaft led to a large, circular room. Along the sides of the corridor shallow nests had been scooped out to serve as beds. It was a comfortable dwelling place, dry and warm but dark. Wu and the cook established a kitchen at the entrance, where the smoke from the fire was drawn up and out through a chimney-like opening in the ceiling.

Ken was delighted. "I've always wanted to live in a cave," he said. "I feel like Neanderthal Man. Maybe if we're lucky we'll see a rhinoceros, or a bison or a tiger roaming about. It seems as though something strange ought to happen."

Benton smiled. "Probably those animals were here half a million years ago. I'd give a lot to go fossil-hunting in Yunnan. We've gone over some wonderful-looking sediments—Pleistocene probably. They're sure to contain bones. Oh, well, we can't do everything. That's one thing about science you'll have to remember, Ken. Every trip opens so many fascinating glimpses of other fields that you are always tempted to leave your specialty and spread yourself too thin. I'm a zoologist,

THE GREAT GORGE OF THE YANGTZE RIVER

but I'd love to study these aboriginal tribes. It seems criminal to be here, at a good deal of expense, and miss the opportunity; also the geology and paleontology and botany couldn't be more interesting. The distribution of animal life is often dependent upon the flora. If we could consider the two together we'd really understand it. But if we dabbled in several sciences we wouldn't have time to do a creditable job in any one.

"I'm convinced that the exploration of the future is to take a group of specialists into the field together. Then each one would complement the other and make the discoveries in every branch of science broader and more accurate and valuable. This idea has been in my mind for a long time. Someday I'm going to do it, and that day won't be too far away."

Ken listened with fascinated interest. "I'd give anything to go with you, Jack."

"Maybe you can if you get your basic academic training first. You can't be a good scientific explorer without it."

"I know that. But it is going to be tough to settle down to college after this trip."

"Not so tough as you think. You know what you want to do with your life. You will be giving yourself thorough preparation and working toward a goal. You can do college in three years if you want to study hard enough."

"But you didn't finish college before you started work in Asia."

"That's true. I was just out of school, as you are. Alex Chapin offered to take me with him on an expedition to Manchuria. When I returned I entered Columbia University as a special student. I'd have a few months in college and then be off on another expedition. It took me five years to get my bachelor's degree, even with credits for field work. Then I registered for graduate study in the same way. I'll come up for my Doctor of Philosophy degree as soon as I've finished some resident requirements."

"Why couldn't I do as you did?"

"You could, of course, but I wouldn't recommend it. If I were doing it over again I'd go through my undergraduate study continuously. There are many reasons. One of them is that field work makes you restless. Also, when you return from an expedition you want to describe and publish your material as soon as possible. It is a nuisance to have to go back into college. Your heart isn't in it, for your collections pull you like a magnet. Studying the specimens you got yourself, and seeing what laws of nature they demonstrate, is almost as exciting as getting them in the field."

Just then Latunga appeared in the entrance of the cavern. He had pushed the jacket off his shoulders, and the upper half of his body shone like polished mahogany. In the flickering firelight he seemed to be the traditional cave man.

Jack called to him. "Where do we go from here?"

The Moso smiled and lighted his little pipe. "There is," he said, "a great forest five days' travel to the north. It's a wonderful place in a low, deep valley. Once I hunted there, and I killed a 'horse deer.' Its horns were like the branches of a tree. I sold them for a hundred dollars at the drug shop in Li-chiang where I buy the poison for my arrows. The Chinese grind them up and make them into medicine. Also in that forest there are big gray monkeys, much like those on the high mountain where the snow leopard lives. There are yellow and black leopards there too. You would find many small creatures for your traps."

"That sounds good," Benton said. "We'll go."

"What is a horse deer?" Ken asked.

"It's an elk, or wapiti, probably *Cervus macneilli* or a related species. The Asiatic wapiti are not well known. They represent the ancestral group from which our American wapiti migrated. Ours has become bigger than any of the known Asiatic forms and has heavier antlers. This one Latunga speaks of might well be a new species. None have been taken from this part of Yunnan."

"What about the monkey?"

"I'd guess it was a langur. The group has more than fifty species that range from the high, bare mountains of Tibet all the way down to Burma and India. In some parts of India they're sacred. Although they do a good deal of damage to crops, the natives don't dare kill them.

"It is just possible we might find golden monkeys there too. That's a beautiful animal with a long golden mane. Until nineteen-eleven, when the Manchu Dynasty lost the throne of China, only the emperor could own their skins because their color is the imperial yellow. Most of the specimens in museums came from the forests of Szechuan, east of here, but their range might extend into Yunnan. We are pretty certain to get a different fauna in the valley."

Two mornings later the expedition climbed by a tortuous trail up the face of the rock wall and struck northward along the rim of the Yangtze gorge. For three days they followed it, reveling in the grandeur of the gigantic chasm.

The valley to which they were bound, Latunga said, lay off the main road into Tibet. To reach it they must cross a high pass, which at this time of the year would be cold. That, they discovered, was an understatement. The pass *was* cold, *very* cold indeed!

A faint trail led straight up a precipitous mountainside. Obviously it had not been used for years. First came a mixed forest, then a dense jungle of dwarf bamboo. Tangled brush and fallen logs continually barred the way. Every few yards they had to stop and lift the loads over a barrier or cut a passage through wirelike thickets.

The bamboo ended at an altitude of 13,000 feet, and low, spreading rhododendrons took its place. They were worse than the bamboo. Sinking into holes, bruising legs on hidden rocks, twisting and turning among a maze of ropelike branches, the men and mules could barely make progress. Beyond the rhododendrons the mountainside rose bare and bleak, covered only with dry grass and patches of snow.

Late in the afternoon the exhausted caravan dragged itself to the summit of the pass. The aneroid barometer registered 16,000 feet. This was the highest they had been. Jack and Ken found it difficult to do their share of camp work because of the thin air. Even the Mosos and the *mafus* were affected. A bitterly cold wind swept across the open summit. It was impossible to keep warm. Everyone hunted for fuel, but only enough twigs and roots could be found to make two miserable fires.

"This," said Benton, "is a fair taste of what we'll get in spring when we reach the snow-leopard country. But we'll be better prepared for it then, and also more acclimated to the high altitudes. Since we left Lichiang we haven't been lower than nine thousand feet. Already I'm getting used to it. Aren't you, Ken?"

"Yes, definitely. It doesn't bother me too much if I do everything in slow motion. By the way, when I was hunting fuel over there to the left I saw a lot of little runways. They are like the runways of *Microtus* on the Snow Mountain. Shouldn't we set some traps? I would think that whatever we got up here ought to be new species."

"Yes, I saw the runways too. Let's each of us take twenty

traps and see who gets the biggest haul. At this altitude and with the Yangtze River between us and the Snow Mountain, the small mammals are bound to be different."

Ken started out with his bag of traps but came back at once for a hatchet. The earth was so solidly frozen that he had to chip out space in the little tunnels for his traps. By the time the bag was empty his teeth were chattering with cold.

Wu and the cook had managed to make some hot pea soup, although at that altitude it took a long time to cook. Ken thought nothing had ever tasted so good.

"I can hardly wait to run my traps in the morning," he said. "Collecting small mammals surely is fun."

Benton laughed. "You've got 'collectitis,' Ken. I am glad to say you won't recover—ever. The disease gets worse the longer you live. It really takes possession of you. Wherever you are, if you see a mossy log, or an old root or a tunnel in the grass, you'll itch to get a trap there and find out what little beasts are running about.

"One of the great collectors of fifty years ago was Major Edgar A. Mearns. He was an army surgeon but a naturalist by avocation. At that time the natural history of our West was very little known. Dr. Mearns got himself assigned to a regiment that was fighting Indians in Arizona. Wherever he happened to be, he put out traps for small mammals and collected birds, even though he continually risked his scalp.

"One day when his troop was on reconnaissance Mearns wandered too far from camp. He was on his knees, setting a trap at a gopher hole, when an arrow whizzed by two inches from his head and plunked into the ground. As he jumped up another cut the flesh of his left arm. The doctor swung up his rifle and fired just as an Indian rose from behind a rock. The bullet caught him right in the head, for Mearns was a dead shot.

"The Apache was alone. Apparently he was a scout, reconnoitering the camp. Dr. Mearns tied a handkerchief about his arm and went on setting his traps as though nothing had happened.

"Finally his commanding officer ordered him not to go beyond the bounds of the post. He didn't want to lose a good surgeon for the sake of a few mice or ground squirrels. Mearns trapped and collected birds all over the West. One of his most productive trips was when he joined the United States-Mexican Boundary Survey. A good many birds and mammals are named for him. He used to send most of his collections to the United States National Museum in Washington."

"Did you ever meet him?" Ken asked.

"Yes, twice. He was on the small side, about five feet nine, with a big mustache and a soft voice. The first time I saw him was at a meeting of the American Ornithologists Union at Harvard. The professional naturalists—like Dr. J. A. Allen and C. Hart Merriam and Dr. E. W. Nelson—were all very fond of him. They got him to telling stories one night. His experiences were terribly exciting, but he told them in the most matter-of-fact way, as though they were nothing unusual."

Ken and Jack talked until late, for it was cold even in their sleeping bags. The *mafus* and Mosos stayed up all night, moving about to keep from freezing. With a flashlight the little cook and Latunga roamed the mountain top, trying to find enough fuel to keep the fires alive, but they had slim pickings.

In the first gray light of dawn the camp was on the move. Ken brought in twelve mammals from his twenty traps. Jack topped him with eighteen. Most of the specimens were a new

species of white-bellied meadow mouse, but there was a re-
markable shrew with a long, curved proboscis—also two
lovely silver moles.

Benton was delighted. "It was worth spending an uncom-
fortable night to get these things," he said, "but I guess no one
but a collector would think so."

XII. Ken Lewis Becomes a God

THE opposite side of the pass was tough work, but the trail turned sharply downhill. By noon the caravan had descended six thousand feet and was back again in the golden sunshine of early autumn. The path began to show signs of recent use. It followed a rushing stream in the bottom of a narrow, heavily wooded ravine. Suddenly the sides broke away, giving entrance to a beautiful valley. Fifteen or twenty mud houses nestled against a hillside just beyond the edge of the forest.

Benton was walking well in front of the caravan with Ken and Latunga. As the men emerged from the ravine they saw a dozen tall felt-caped figures rushing to the houses.

Latunga stopped. "This," he said, "I do not like. These people are not Mosos. They are Lolos. Not all Lolos are friendly. We must be careful."

Benton gasped. "Lolos! That's bad. We're in the middle of them. What shall we do?"

"Wait here and stop the caravan. I'll talk with them. They all speak Tibetan. I can too. Maybe it will be all right."

Latunga walked toward the largest house with his arms above his head. Then he halted, opened his mouth, and extended his tongue in the Tibetan greeting. For what seemed a long time to Benton, nothing happened. At last out of the door stepped a tall young man with a black turban wrapped about his head. He carried a long-barreled gun. A thin wisp of smoke curled up from a ropelike fuse at the stock. The Lolo put out his tongue. Latunga walked forward. Benton and Ken could see gun barrels projecting from the windows and doors of several houses. For a time the two men talked; then Latunga beckoned to Jack and Ken. After laying their guns on the ground, they walked forward, sticking out their tongues as Latunga had done. The tall Lolo returned the greeting by extending his tongue an incredible distance.

Latunga said, "These people will be friendly, I think. They are suspicious, for no one has come over the mountain for a very long time. This man is chief of the village. He speaks Tibetan and a little Chinese—not well, but I can understand him. I think you can too."

While Latunga was talking the tall Lolo had been staring at Jack and Ken. Astonishment, incredulity, and finally curiosity, registered on his face. Benton spoke to him in Chinese. For a few moments his eyes remained blank. Then he seemed to realize that the words had meaning and that it was something he could understand. He returned the greeting briefly. Then, bluntly: "Where do you come from? I have never seen people like you before. Why do you come to our valley?" He talked haltingly in a peculiar dialect.

"Latunga, tell him we live in a country far away across a big sea; that we are here to shoot and trap wild animals for their skins. Ask if there are hunters in this village who will help us. We wish to be friends and would like to stay for a while."

Latunga spoke rapidly in Tibetan. The Lolo nodded and extended his tongue. From Benton he accepted a cigarette.

"The chief says all the men here are hunters and they live on game. If you wish you may stay. Over there near the stream is a place to put the tents."

Benton waved his hand, and the caravan wound slowly out of the ravine into the valley. As the loads were being removed a dozen natives emerged from the houses and gathered in a silent group. They were tall, fine-looking men with high-bridged noses, thin lips, and comparatively light complexions. Their straight features seemed almost Caucasian.

The Lolos stared at Ken and Jack. Benton smiled and pulled up his sleeve, showing the white skin of his arm. Murmurs of amazement ran through the crowd. Latunga laughed. "They are just as surprised as I was when I saw you first. They can't understand what kind of people you are. Your light-colored eyes are what interest them most. It was the same with me. They wonder if you can see well."

Several of the Lolos had crossbows, but others carried guns. These were most extraordinary-looking weapons. Latunga asked the young chief to let Ken examine his. With some reluctance the Lolo passed it to him. The barrel was six feet long with a short stock, shaped like a golfstick. A powder fuse projected from a hole in the side of the barrel, and just behind it, on the butt, was fastened a forked spring. At his waist the chief carried a long coil of rope, the burning end of which was held in the crotched spring. When about to shoot, the man placed the weapon against his cheek and aimed. Then he pressed the spring, so that the burning rope's end touched the fuse. It was about as primitive a gun as could be devised. By no possibility would it be effective at more than forty yards. Latunga said the weapons came from Tibet.

Ken brought out his 6.5-mm. Mannlicher and a little .22-caliber Winchester repeater. He showed the Lolos the cartridges and how they fitted in the magazine.

Latunga said to Jack, "It wouldn't be a bad idea to let them see what your guns can do. They seem friendly, and I am sure they are, else I wouldn't agree that we stay here. But still they are Lolos. One never knows."

Jack nodded.

Latunga told the chief that the young stranger wanted to show them how his rifles worked. Would he put five small pieces of wood on that stump? Latunga pointed to a stump a hundred and fifty yards away. The Lolo smiled increduously. Nevertheless, he set up a row of three-inch chips.

Latunga made an excellent master of ceremonies and thoroughly enjoyed the role. He explained importantly that the young stranger would shoot five bullets, one right after the other, and that the five chips would fly apart—that if each one were an animal, even as big as a leopard or a horse deer, it would be dead.

Ken threw shells into the Mannlicher and fired rapidly. All the chips disappeared in a shower of splinters. The Lolos stared, speechless with amazement. Then they gathered about the stump, examining the wood ripped open by the high-powered bullets.

Benton said, "Good so far. But we're not through with you yet, Ken. Take the twenty-two and give them an exhibition of really high-class shooting."

Latunga cut some pieces of wood about an inch square. These he gave to the chief. "Throw one high in the air," he said, "and the young stranger will break it with the little bullet."

The Lolo tossed up the tiny block. Ken shattered it before the chunk had risen ten feet.

"Now throw two at the same time." Ken split one on the way up and the other as it fell. Then he broke three. The Lolos could only shake their heads in silent wonder. This was magic!

A hawk was circling just above the treetops. "It it comes low enough, kill it with your revolver, Ken. Let them see how fast you can draw and shoot. That'll be the final touch."

Latunga explained to the Lolos what was about to happen. Ken stood with his arms hanging loosely at his sides. Apparently he was not watching the hawk, but as it swooped down just above their heads he whirled, drew his revolver, and fired in one swift motion. The bird started to fall, but before it touched the ground two more bullets had torn it almost apart.

Latunga tried to be nonchalant, but he made a poor job of it. His face was radiant, for he was inordinately proud of Ken. "The older stranger can shoot just as well," he said. Jack smiled and walked into their tent with Ken. "Thank heaven I don't have to try," he remarked. "I'd ruin all your good work. If I lived to be a thousand years old I couldn't shoot like that. I don't wonder the natives are impressed. Every time I see you draw and fire that revolver it seems miraculous."

"Mostly practice. I've worked at it ever since I was five years old. I had a toy pistol, and I used to stand in front of a mirror by the hour, drawing and snapping. I'd pretend I was

Wild Bill Hickok and that I'd have to get my man before he got me. When Dad gave me a real gun he fixed up a shooting gallery in our basement and one in the back yard. I used to work there for hours every day. I spent all my allowance for ammunition. After a while Dad saw I might be really good and he got serious about it. He had an instructor come out twice a week. I learned a lot from him. One thing he said I never forgot. 'I can teach you the basic rules of shooting. But that will be of no use unless you practice every day. You can be exactly as good as you want to be. It just depends upon how much you are willing to work at it.' I haven't had any practice at this trick shooting, and I was a little worried today. But it turned out all right."

"I'll say it did," Jack remarked dryly.

Just then Latunga appeared in the tent door. He put his arm affectionately about Ken's shoulders. "What you have done," he said, "is wonderful. The Lolos believe you are sent by the hunting gods to this valley because tomorrow is their yearly feast and sacrifice. They are sure it means the gods are pleased with them. They ask if you will take part in the ceremony. It will be at a big rock below the village just at sunrise."

Ken looked at Jack, who nodded. "Tell them the young god will be glad to accept their invitation. Ask them, too, if the women wouldn't like to see our camp."

Half an hour later twenty or more women arrived with as many men and children. Some of the girls were really pretty. They had graceful figures, laughing brown eyes, and rosy cheeks. There was none of the shyness of Chinese women, and their dress was extraordinary—flat black turbans, short jackets, and long skirts with huge flounces. It gave them a curiously old-fashioned look, quite out of harmony with the metal neck-bands, earrings, and heavy bracelets all of them wore.

Benton had brought from America several dozen small steel mirrors. Ken presented one to each of the women, to their great delight. They asked Latunga if the young god would let them see his white skin. Ken pulled up his sleeve. The women oh-ed and ah-ed. Then one said, "Can it be that he is white like that all over?"

"Yes, he is," Latunga said.

Benton laughed. "Open your shirt, Ken, and give the gals a thrill."

Ken blushed furiously. "I'll be darned if I will. They can take Latunga's word for it. I've been on exhibition long enough. Jack, show them a flashlight. They'll get a kick out of that. Maybe it will take their minds off me."

The flashlight had the desired effect. That a spot of light could appear and disappear in the black tube, with no visible fire, was unbelievable. The little portable Victrola almost dispersed the gathering permanently. A musical record excited only curiosity. But when a human voice issued from the box, that was black magic! Every man, woman, and child ran as though the devil were after him. They ventured back only when the "devil box" had been put away.

Next morning, in the gray light of dawn, Latunga and the chief arrived at the tent. As Ken emerged the Lolo kowtowed deeply, much to Ken's embarrassment. Jack grinned. "You're a god now, and don't you forget it. You'll get used to being divine after a while. It will have advantages."

Two hundred yards below the last house of the village, they came to a small secluded amphitheater. The sides rose steeply to a jagged skyline of granite crags. Near the center stood a low flat rock, like a temple altar. At one side half a dozen fires gleamed under iron pots. Already every man, woman, and child of the village was sitting on the grass about the rock. The chief asked Ken to stand by its side.

Just as the sun shot its first golden shafts into the amphitheater, the chief advanced. He placed seven lighted incense sticks about a shallow depression in the rock's surface. A tall Lolo brought him a great white rooster. While it flapped disconsolately, the chief slit the neck and dripped blood in three concentric circles about the depression. Then, after opening the breast, he removed the heart and placed it on a broad green leaf. This he presented to Ken with both hands. Ken knew from the Moso ceremony what he was supposed to do. With no hesitation he popped it in his mouth.

The chief half filled the basin in the rock with blood from the rooster. Each of the men came forward singly, dipped his fingers in the blood, and smeared his forehead. Then he turned and kowtowed three times to Ken. Latunga followed the example of the Lolos and made his obeisance as the others had done. Jack said later, "That wasn't only a gesture, Ken. He really worships you."

To his surprise, Ken did not feel embarrassed. The ceremony was strange and barbaric, but he could not close his mind to the religious fervor that radiated from everyone, men and women alike. They believed implicitly that he had been sent by the hunting gods to show favor to the village. That gave them a childlike confidence and happiness which anyone might envy.

As the ceremony ended, all the Lolos gathered about the cooking pots filled with boiled goat's meat. Brass pitchers of buttered tea and wooden bowls of *tsampa* were passed to Jack and Ken by the girls. The food was good, and they did not need to pretend to eat.

"You did nobly with the heart, Ken," Benton said. "Did you swallow it whole?"

"No, I've got it in my pocket. I slipped it out of my mouth when no one was looking."

"Get rid of it as soon as we leave here, and for goodness' sake don't let Latunga see you. He'd be crushed."

When the last scrap of goat's meat had vanished the chief escorted Jack and Ken back to their tent. Latunga was very happy. The ceremony, he said, had been a great success. Now they could have anything they wanted, not only from these Lolos but from any others whom they might meet. The chief would give them a passport for all his people.

XIII. Benton Looks at Death

THE Lolo village was only a dozen miles from the great
valley of which Latunga had told them. There, the chief
said, they should find good hunting. He would go with them
himself and take three or four of his best men.

The caravan moved out the next morning. A trail led steeply
down the mountain to the floor of a subtropical valley. The
forest was magnificent. Immense spreading trees stretched up
more than a hundred and fifty feet, their interlaced branches
forming a canopy thick as a ceiling. A smothering mass of
streaming gray moss, creepers, and parasitic plants clothed
every tree trunk; from the lower limbs thousands of ropelike

vines swayed back and forth. Even the noonday sun gave only a somber twilight beneath the trees. The air felt soft and damp and warm.

Ken was amazed. "It doesn't seem possible there could be anything like this so near Tibet. It's the way I've always imagined Borneo to be. And two nights ago we were in winter!"

"Well, you see, Yunnan Province actually is quite far south in latitude. The name means 'South of the Clouds.' The northern part is cool because it is so high. We've seldom been lower than nine thousand feet."

The Lolo chief directed them along the valley to an open space under two great trees, near a sparkling stream. Turning to Ken, he spread his hands in a gesture that asked, "Is this all right?"

Ken put up his thumb and smiled. "It couldn't be more beautiful. Latunga, tell him I am very pleased."

Jack grinned. "I'm glad the god approves."

The tents were up and camp made in half an hour. The Lolos built a small fire beside the stream a dozen yards away and boiled their tea. Each one carried a leather pouch full of *tsampa*, and a chunk of brick tea. That would be their only food until an animal was killed.

In the afternoon Ken stayed in camp to write up data on the collections, while Latunga went with Benton to set a line of traps. The little Moso had become greatly interested in small mammals, for they opened a new world of nature to him. Before, he had known only a few of the little creatures that made the mysterious night noises to which he loved to listen when he lay in a pile of leaves or beside a rock. Now he had learned what they were and how they lived.

Benton had put out fifty traps, and he and Latunga were on

their way back to camp when suddenly the forest rang with a strange, half-human whoop. Latunga grabbed Jack's arm. "Those are the gray monkeys—the ones I told you about. They're coming this way."

The monkeys seemed far off at first, but their voices sounded louder and clearer every moment. The men slipped from one tree to another, moving forward only when the animals called. It was an exciting stalk.

While they were still fifty yards away, a huge gray monkey leaped out of a treetop just as Benton stepped from behind a bush. The animal saw Jack instantly. For a long moment it hung suspended by one arm, its head thrust forward, staring intently. Then, after launching itself into the air as though shot from a catapult, the monkey caught a branch twenty feet away, swung to another, and simply flew through the treetops. Without a sound save the swish of branches and splash after splash in the leaves, the herd lost itself in the forest.

Jack was disconcerted. He had not dreamed that the monkeys could travel so fast, and he felt rather foolish. It seemed like a sound idea to smoke a pipe and talk it over with Latunga. They were on the brink of a deep gorge filled with a tangle of vines and creepers and thorny plants. The sides dropped away in sheer walls to a torrent of white water leaping and foaming over a chaos of rocks and boulders far below.

Their pipes were hardly lighted when, far away, the faint whoops of another herd of langurs floated up the valley. The monkeys were coming fast, directly toward the men. In a few moments they saw the gray forms racing through the treetops on the opposite side of the ravine. Finally the herd stopped and began to feed.

A big fellow swung out on a branch, hanging by one hand while he picked a cluster of leaves with the other. At two

hundred yards, he was a small mark. Jack rested his little
Mannlicher on a stump and began to shoot. The first bullet cut
a twig about the monkey's head, but the animal didn't move.
At the second shot he dropped heavily into the vines. Another
monkey ran along the branch and peered down where the first
one had fallen. When Benton fired, it pitched headlong off the
limb. Latunga grinned, holding up his thumb. Silence for a
few seconds; then three big langurs leaped into view from the
top of a tall tree. Silhouetted against a patch of sky, they made
perfect targets. Jack missed them twice. Like gray shadows
they faded into the jungle.

For ten minutes the men sat motionless, hoping to catch a
glimpse of a swaying branch. Suddenly Latunga heard a faint
rustling in the low tree under which they were crouching.
Grabbing Jack by the arm, he yelled, "There's one—right over
us!"

They looked up into the blazing eyes of a huge monkey. It
wasn't fifteen feet above their heads. Latunga fired with the
shotgun. The animal stopped, pivoted on one long arm, swung
back, and dropped almost on the Moso's head. Of all the trees
in the forest they had chosen to sit under the one where the
monkey was hiding!

Getting around the head of the ravine to where the other
monkeys had fallen was difficult and dangerous. It was like
circling a wall covered with vines and thorny plants. They
were an hour making two hundred yards in a shooting line.
Latunga found the big monkey right where he had dropped.
The other lay twenty feet below in a tangle of vines and
creepers.

With the carbine slung across his back, Benton worked
down the steep slope. The rock-face was covered with a thin
layer of earth, supporting a dense growth of vegetation. Sud-

denly a vine to which Jack was clinging gave way. Beginning to slide, he grabbed frantically at a bush, but it stripped off. Faster and faster he went, dragging a mass of creepers. Whatever he touched tore loose. Only two more yards to the rim of the precipice! A hundred feet below lay the jagged rocks of the stream bed.

The rifle on his back saved his life. It jammed in a projecting ledge but left him spreadeagled as though crucified. He was sick from terror. Everything went black for a few seconds. Then, as from a great distance, he heard Latunga's voice. The words finally penetrated his numbed brain. "Don't move. I'll come for you."

How he could come Benton didn't know, but he had complete confidence in the little Moso.

For ten minutes he hung there, almost afraid to breathe. Then, at his left side, Latunga spoke quietly. "I've got a vine. Don't move when I slide it under your back." He felt Latunga push a ropelike vine around his body and tie it over his breast in a figure-eight knot.

"It's very strong," the Moso said. "You needn't fear. Now twist to the left and loosen the rifle. Let yourself hang. That's right. Now turn on your face. Pull up your knees against the rock. Good. Now your feet. Walk up the vine the way I'm doing."

Jack did as he was told. Latunga climbed beside him on another vine. Digging his bare toes into the crevices, he went up like a monkey. Benton's boots made it more difficult, but the hobnails held against the rock. In less than a minute both men reached the tree about which the vines were fastened.

Jack slumped on the ground. He felt weak and a little sick. The path he had torn down the rock-face through the tangle of vegetation lay stark and bare. It made him shudder. Had it not been for Latunga his body would be lying crumpled on the rocks at the bottom of the chasm.

The Moso patted him on the shoulder and smiled in sympathy. "You'll be all right in a little while. Rest here. I'll get the monkey."

Benton looked into his eyes. "Someday, Latunga, maybe I'll be able to pay my debt to you."

With the rope-vine still about his waist, Latunga recovered the langur. It proved to be a big gray female. To their surprise, a tiny baby was clinging tightly to the long hair between the forelegs. Apparently it had not impeded the mother in her leaps through the treetops.

The infant was bright orange-red. It couldn't have been more than a few days old. Jack wrapped it in his handkerchief. With only its queer little wizened face and blue eyes visible, it looked amazingly like a human baby until its long tail suddenly flopped into sight.

The small creature was an excellent sedative for Benton's shaken nerves. He played with it while Latunga made a sling from vines and fastened the three dead monkeys to his shoulders. Then they worked slowly through the forest back to camp.

Ken was horrified at Jack's story. "How lucky that Latunga was with you instead of me," he said. "Maybe I wouldn't have thought of the vines. Latunga always seems to know what to do, no matter what happens."

"That's true, but he has lived all his life in the forest. Probably something like this has occurred before. He was as quiet and efficient as though he had done it a dozen times."

"Do you remember my telling you about the serow I killed at the White Water—the one that fell into the ravine?"

"Yes, you said the Mosos made a ladder out of vines."

"They did, and it must have been fifty feet long. They went up and down it like squirrels. And they pulled the serow up without any trouble. They used only one kind of vine. It was tough and pliable. They could tie it in knots just like a rope."

Jack felt something stir in his pocket and suddenly remembered the baby monkey. Ken was much amused at its wizened human-like face and orange-colored body. The little animal opened its pink mouth and mewed.

Jack got a glass dropper from the medicine kit. "You take over, Ken. Feed him with diluted condensed milk. He doesn't look much like the old ones, does he? I've seen skins of immature langurs in the museum. Apparently the red coat goes off slowly. The tail is the last part to change."

The Lolos were examining the dead monkeys with great interest. Latunga showed them the bullet holes. He demonstrated the distance at which the animals had been shot, and stretched it a hundred yards. The chief looked at Benton with some of the awe that had been reserved for Ken alone.

That night, while they were smoking beside the fire, Latunga told them what he had learned about these Lolos. It was a story much like that of Daniel Boone in Kentucky. Some "tens of years" ago, Latunga said, the young chief's grandfather had left Lolo Land. There he was head man of a village. Because it was a happy community, more people came. The village grew in size. The young chief's grandfather felt the place was crowded. One day he left with only his gun and crossbow, and a dog. His eyes were turned westward toward the great mountains of Tibet.

For almost a year he wandered, crossing the Yangtze River into forests where he saw few human beings. His food was the animals he killed and wild berries and fruit and roots. In the spring he discovered this valley. He called it the "Valley of the Flowers." There was much game, but he had always lived in the hills. So he climbed out of the valley and came to the place where the Lolos now had their village.

For three months he stayed there, going down into the Valley of the Flowers to hunt. He was very happy. This spot, he decided, was where he wished to live and die. So he returned to Lolo Land. He told some of his friends about what he had found. Six families, all those of hunters, decided to emigrate with him to the new country. Eventually others came.

After the old man died the young chief's father became head man. Then his son inherited the position. He had absolute authority of life or death over the community. His word was law, according to Lolo custom.

Twice a year two or three of the men went north to a small town on the Tibetan frontier, to trade their skins and furs for brick tea, tobacco, and cloth. While the young chief had been there the previous month, he had heard that Chinese soldiers had killed fifteen or twenty Lolos who were on a hunting expedition outside their own territory in Szechuan, not many days' travel from the valley. The Lolos didn't like that. They got a lot of their people together and attacked the Chinese city where the soldiers were quartered. Many of them were killed. So now all Lolos, wherever they were, had to be very careful.

When the expedition appeared at the entrance to the valley, the chief was afraid they were Chinese come to destroy his village. The Lolos were ready to fight. Then he saw Benton and Ken. He couldn't imagine what kind of people they were. He had never heard of anybody like them. After the Lolos had seen Ken shoot, everyone knew he must be one of the hunting gods come to the annual ceremony. No one but a god could shoot like that. They were very happy about it.

When Latunga finished his story Jack said, "I don't wonder they figured it out that way. In their minds it's quite simple and natural. You've made a pretty good set-up for us, Ken. The Lolos will work like everything, and this place must be full of game. Tomorrow you go out with them and show what a real live god can do."

He yawned. "I've had a pretty tough afternoon. I feel like a sucked orange. I'm going to bed. Good night."

Ken and Latunga smoked a last pipe. The Moso poked up the fire and wriggled into a pile of leaves beside it. Ken left the tent flaps open. It's a good life, he thought as his mind drifted into sleep. I like being a god.

XIV. Jack Pays His Debt

"LATUNGA thinks there is a good chance of getting a wapiti," Benton said at breakfast. "They are in this low valley for only a few weeks in the winter. The Lolos don't kill many because their guns can't shoot far enough. They only snare them now and then. The wapiti is their prize animal. If they get a big pair of antlers in the velvet they can trade them with the Tibetans for enough tea, tobacco, and cloth to last the whole village several months. The Tibetans sell the antlers to the Chinese for medicine. The antlers won't be in velvet now, of course, but it would give us great face if the young hunting god got one on the first day. That would prove you were divine. Not that there is any doubt of it in the Lolo minds—or Latunga's either. As for me, I'd rather have you as you are."

Ken laughed. "Well, I don't feel a bit divine, but I'd surely like to kill a wapiti. Dad had planned to take me on an elk hunt in Wyoming last year, but he got sick and couldn't go. I was terribly disappointed. By the way, why do you always call them 'wapiti'? I thought their proper name was 'elk.'"

"It isn't really. It is a confusion of terms that started when the first colonists came to America. Elk is the name in Europe for the animal with broad, palmated antlers that we call moose. When the first white men saw the big American deer, they spoke of it as elk, even though it didn't have palmated antlers. Elk was the only very large deer they knew. Later they discovered that there was another American animal that had palmated antlers just like the European elk, and that the Indian name for it was 'moose.' The Indian term for the animal they had at first called elk was 'wapiti.' So, in order to avoid confusion, naturalists adopted the name wapiti for the big deer, with branching antlers, of America and Asia. The Chinese call it *ma lou*, or horse deer. But the word 'elk' had already become so fixed in conversation and literature that it could not be eliminated. Does my double talk make sense to you?"

"Yes. Our moose is elk to the Europeans, and our elk is wapiti to naturalists."

"That's right. Latunga suggests that you go with the chief while he and the dogs drive a patch of heavy cover where the wapiti lie up during the day. The Lolos know where they'll run. You'd better use your nine-millimeter Mannlicher. The six-five is a little light for those big fellows."

Latunga had already left with three Lolos and the hounds, when the chief came to get Ken. They made their way for about a mile down a shallow valley to the edge of a parklike

meadow dotted with trees. Behind them a narrow glade cut
deep into the wall of forest. The Lolo indicated that the deer
would come down the runway and cross the meadow into
the thick woods on the other side.

A clump of bushes made an excellent blind. Ken settled himself beside the chief where they could look into the runway.
A troop of langurs swung about in the treetops on the edge of
the forest. The sight of the big gray monkeys brought Benton's
narrow escape to his mind. What would he have done if Jack
had been killed? It was too terrible to think about! How fortunate that they had found Latunga in Lichiang! Every day
Ken became fonder of him. The Moso was like an older
brother. Before he came to China he never would have believed he could feel that way about a native. But no one could
help liking and respecting Latunga. He was so direct and
simple and honest, and so thoughtful and sympathetic. That
came, Ken supposed, from living close to nature and her wild
creatures. Latunga's code was one of absolute loyalty. He
would never hesitate to risk his life if anyone he cared for were
in danger, or to fulfill any obligation. It would be hard to say
good-by to him when they left Yunnan!

Suddenly, in the treetops, the monkeys began to chatter
excitedly. The chief touched Ken's arm. Faint, and very far
away, the thin cry of hounds drifted through the trees. Ken
rested on one knee with the rifle cocked. For a full minute he
waited. Then a dim form, moving swiftly and followed by
another, took shape in the gloom of the narrow forest avenue.

On the instant a great stag burst into the open. Head out,
with branching antlers lying back against his shoulders, he
came on in tremendous bounds. A doe, almost as large, ran
close on the stag's heels. They were less than a hundred yards
away.

Ken never forgot that picture. Every detail was indelibly photographed on his memory. Years later he could still visualize how he had centered the ivory bead of the front sight on the brown shoulder, swung the muzzle forward, and touched the trigger. He could hear the "plunk" of the bullet and see the magnificent animal turn a complete somersault, half burying his antlers in the earth. He could remember throwing the bolt of the rifle, picking up the flying doe through the rear sights, and seeing her go down with a broken neck, like a felled ox.

Never would he forget the wild yell of the young chief as he ran to the dead wapiti—and then how the Lolo, with reverence in his eyes, kowtowed as he stood knee deep in the lush grass.

Ken was still shaking with excitement when the hounds swept out of the woods. Big Red, nose to the ground, ran well in front, with the pack closely bunched behind him. The dogs suddenly put on brakes, piled up in a yelling mass on the dead deer, and began pulling at the carcasses. The Lolo drove them off.

Ken found a package of cigarettes in his pocket and gave one to the chief. He didn't want his pipe then. That was for quiet, peaceful moments. For a time the American boy and the tall Lolo smoked in the happy companionship that comes when two people share a mutual passion. Ken could understand little of the chief's strange Chinese dialect, but there was no need for words. Every few moments the native drew a long breath, put up his thumb, and shook his head as though unable to believe what his eyes had seen.

Before their cigarettes were finished, Latunga and the three Lolos dashed out of the forest glade and across the meadow. The chief spoke rapidly, telling them what had happened.

They examined the little bullet holes with amazement; then each kowtowed in turn.

Ken knew Benton would want to photograph and measure the animals before they were skinned, so he asked Latunga to bring Jack from camp.

In less than an hour Jack appeared, grinning happily. "You really did a job for us, Ken. I feel as though I ought to kowtow to you too. Latunga is ready to burst with pride. He says the Lolos couldn't be more impressed. They haven't caught a *ma lou* for three years, and you kill two on the first hunt! I will say it was darned good shooting."

"They were awfully easy shots, but I was lucky to get each of them down with one bullet. I was never more excited in my life. I'll always remember how they looked when they leaped out of that runway!"

Jack examined the deer with enormous interest. "I can hardly wait to go over the descriptions of the other Asiatic wapiti," he said. "It might be a new species. No big deer has been described from anywhere near this region. How much they look like our American wapiti! But you see the antlers are straighter and the main beam doesn't turn downward at the end. Of course, our wapiti are migrants from Asia."

He took photographs and a series of measurements. Then he said to Latunga, "Tell the Lolos we're ready to skin the *ma lou*. They can take over now."

The chief opened the deer and carefully removed the hearts. These he presented to Ken on a layer of green leaves. Latunga told him to slice off a small bit from each one and eat it, then to pass the hearts back to the Lolo. They would be taken to the village and divided equally among all the hunters. Thus, each one would share in the good fortune the Young God had brought to their valley.

Ken swallowed his bits with no hesitation. By this time the
feel and taste of raw heart wasn't too disagreeable. "I might
even like it," he said to Jack, "if I could season it with salt and
pepper. Probably when we get home I'll demand my piece of
raw heart every day."

Benton cut out the two long strips of fillet from the back
of the doe. These were for use in camp. Then, with Latunga
translating, Ken told the chief, in rather a grand manner, that
he wished to present the rest of the meat to the village.

Jack grinned appreciatively. "You do the god act very well,
Ken. You'll have a hard time being mortal again when we leave
the Lolos."

The chief thanked him, and the natives set to work. In half
an hour the bones of both wapiti were bare. One of the Lolos
went to the edge of the forest and returned, trailing ropes
of vines. Each man wove himself a basket, which he loaded
with meat and slung over his shoulders.

Between them, Benton, Ken, and Latunga were able to carry
the two skins and heads. They spent the rest of the morning
cleaning and salting the hides.

In the afternoon Jack said, "I think it would be a good idea
to set some steel traps down by the *ma lou* bones. A beautiful
cat, *Felis temmicki*, is supposed to come from somewhere in
this region. The skins are very rare in collections. I know there
are civets here. I saw their tracks in the mud of the stream.
There ought to be other things too."

"I've heard American skunks called civets. Are these like our
skunks?" Ken asked.

"No, they belong to the family *Viverridæ*. They are pretty,
gray animals, spotted with black, and with a black and white
ringed tail—bigger than a large cat. They live only in Asia and
Africa. A scent gland near the base of the tail gives a strong

musklike odor, but it's not particularly disagreeable—nothing like that of a skunk."

The wapiti bones lay under a low tree. Benton set half a dozen medium-sized steel traps in a circle about the pile. Each one was buried in a shallow pit and covered lightly with leaves and grass. The chains were attached to loose branches or heavy sticks.

"Why don't you stake them down?" Ken asked.

"Because the animal can often work out of the trap if it has something solid to pull against. The drag catches in the grass or bushes and gives as the beast struggles. It seldom goes far."

In camp Jack suggested that Ken set a line of traps for small mammals. "The Lolos won't be back for a day or two. The chief said they were planning a big feast on the *ma lou*. To-morrow I'll roam about with Latunga and have a look at other parts of the valley. Above camp the stream spreads out into a deep pool. I saw fish in it—salamanders and frogs too. We'll have a 'marine day' soon and fill our formalin cans. It will be fun."

"All of it's fun," Ken said. "Only I know so darned little about these things."

"I don't know much either, except in a general way. The day of the old-time naturalist is ended. Fifty years ago every one of the professional naturalists had a pretty good working knowledge of mammals, birds, fish, reptiles, and insects. But now each subject has expanded so greatly that it isn't possible. It's just like medicine. Most city doctors are specialists. They won't touch anything out of their particular field. Country doctors have to generalize a good deal. So do collectors. They have a broader knowledge than the 'closet naturalists' in museums, who stick to their own subjects."

Ken sighed. "When I get home I'll have enough reading to do to last me the rest of my life. Well, I'll get out my trapline. At least I'm beginning to know something about mammals."

In the morning Benton took his rifle and gave Latunga a shotgun. "We'll go down to where the *ma lou* bones are first," he said, "and then into the forest on the other side of the meadow."

When they reached the pile it was obvious that some animal had been there. The grass was torn up and the bones scattered in every direction. Two of the traps were gone. Latunga knelt under the tree to examine the ground. Suddenly, from a low branch above his head, came a coughing snarl. Before he could straighten up, eighty pounds of biting, clawing leopardess landed on his back. The Moso went down, but twisted away from the teeth lunging for his neck. The cat got his right arm near the shoulder in her mouth. He could hear snarling grunts and crunching sounds as she tore his flesh. He caught her throat with his left hand and squeezed hard. Her grip loosened a little when he shut off her wind. He tried to pull his arm free, but she shifted to another hold above the elbow. They rolled over and over. Finally he got on top. He pressed his knees into the animal's breast and heard a rib crack. But he felt himself weakening. Then, suddenly, the gripping teeth relaxed, and, with a convulsive shudder, the raging beast stretched out like a great sleeping cat.

Latunga tried to stand, but his knees gave way. Black patches flickered across his eyes, and he felt sick. Two hands under his arms lifted him up and guided him to a spot in the thick grass, where he lay down. Finally his brain cleared. He saw Jack Benton's face above him.

"Stay quiet, Latunga. I want to fix your arm. You'll be all right soon."

Vaguely, as though from a great distance, the Moso heard the sharp rip of cloth and felt bandages being wound about his shoulder and arm. He was glad not to move.

Half an hour later the Moso sat up. His vitality, like that of a wild animal, cut through the shock and loss of blood. He smiled when Benton asked him how he felt.

Latunga said he felt all right; he'd like a cigarette. While they smoked he asked what had happened.

"When the leopard landed on your back," Jack said, "I couldn't shoot. You and the cat were just a whirling, clawing ball. Sometimes you were on top, and sometimes the leopard. I pulled out my knife and waited for a chance to use it. I only hoped it would come before she sank her teeth in your throat. When you got your knees in her breast I stuck my knife in right behind her foreleg. It went through her lungs into the heart."

Jack drew the leopard over to where Latunga could see it. The beautiful yellow and black animal shone in the sunlight as though washed with gold. On both hind feet two traps were firmly clamped.

"Those," Benton said, "are what saved your life. If her hind claws had been free she would have ripped you apart."

"Well," Latunga remarked laconically, "if she hadn't got her feet in the traps she wouldn't have been here. They're much too small for a leopard. I don't know why I didn't remember when you started out from camp that you might catch one. I know this valley is full of leopards. The time I hunted here I heard them every night. It was all my fault, and it serves me right."

"That," said Jack, "is just what you would say. The question now is how to get you back to camp! Do you think you can walk that far?"

Latunga got to his feet. "Of course I can. My arm doesn't seem to work, but my legs are all right."

Benton made a sling for the torn arm and steadied him on the left side. Latunga stepped out briskly but soon slowed down. His teeth were set, and sweat poured down his face. The shock was wearing off, and his mangled arm hurt terribly.

Camp was barely a mile away, but to Jack it seemed like a hundred miles. It was hard to see the gallant little Moso fight to stay on his feet. But he must get antiseptic on the arm and shoulder as soon as possible. Benton was afraid of blood poisoning. Leopards feed on carrion, and their teeth and claws reek with infectious material.

More than an hour later they dragged themselves into camp. Ken was skinning mice at a table beside the stream. He almost fainted when he saw Latunga, covered with dirt, and with blood oozing through the bandages and what was left of his clothes.

"Fight with a leopard," Jack said. "Get hot water from the cook tent. Tell Wu to bring me a big cloth. I'll give Latunga a shot of morphine before we start to clean him up. He's about done."

Benton untied the bandages he had torn from his shirt. The arm was in bad shape. It looked like a mass of hamburger. He made up a pail of potassium permanganate, ten times standard strength, and with a syringe pumped it into every one of the tooth wounds and claw marks. There were dozens of them— so many that as the antiseptic went into one hole it came out another.

By the time Jack had finished the operation Latunga was

half asleep from the morphine and weakness. He was too drowsy to protest when they helped him to a bed of soft moss in their tent.

"He'll be all right," Benton said, "if we can keep the infection down. That's the only thing to worry about. But these natives have great resistance. They're just like healthy animals. We'll let him sleep and watch his temperature. There is nothing more to be done right now. Let's go down and bring up the leopard. We can carry her easily on a pole."

The place looked like a battlefield, with blood all over the grass, and bones scattered about. Jack showed Ken where the leopard had dropped out of the tree onto Latunga's back.

"How she got rid of the drags and climbed up there with those traps on both her hind feet, I can't imagine. She was the maddest cat you've ever seen. If she hadn't snarled just before she jumped, Latunga would have been a dead man. She'd have caught him by the neck. He looked up and twisted his body as she came down."

Ken thought he had never seen a more beautiful creature or one so lethal. The razor-sharp claws and gleaming teeth were such terrible weapons that it seemed incredible that any man could fight them with his bare hands and live.

Back in camp, Wu reported that Latunga hadn't moved. Jack took his temperature. It was only two degrees above normal.

"I doubt that there'll be any serious infection, but we'll have to watch him all night. It wouldn't show as soon as this."

"Will you let me sit up with him?" Ken asked. "I want to do something for him, and I'll call you if you're needed. I can take his temperature perfectly well."

"Certainly you can. I know how you feel. We've both come to love the little fellow."

Twice that night Latunga roused enough to ask for water. Ken held a cup to his lips and took his temperature. It continued to be almost normal. At daylight Jack relieved him, and Ken went to sleep.

XV. Ordeal by Snake

LATUNGA waked in midmorning. He had slept twenty-two hours. Jack could not find a trace of infection; still he bathed and swabbed the wounds again. The arm and shoulder were red and badly swollen, but the antiseptic, plus an iron constitution, had done its work. The Moso seemed surprisingly strong and insisted on walking about camp. Only when an involuntary spasm of pain crossed his face at some sudden movement did he show signs of his terrible ordeal.

"It is amazing," Benton remarked to Ken, "what these natives can endure. Of course it's because they live a completely natural life. They recover as quickly as a wild animal.

You or I would be out for weeks if we were chewed up the way he is. I'll bet he'll be almost well in a few days."

"Thank God for that," Ken said. "I'd never get over it if anything happened to Latunga."

Before noon the Lolos returned, bringing a basket of eggs and a skin bag of goat's milk. They were amazed at Latunga's escape. The chief said leopards were the most feared of all animals in the valley. Two years ago one of the best hunters of their village had been killed by a leopard not far from this camp. As with Latunga, it had dropped out of a tree onto his shoulders while he was walking up a deer runway. He didn't have a chance to fight. Latunga was a very lucky man. Obviously, the influence of the young hunting god was what had saved his life!

Benton smiled somewhat ruefully. "They might give a little credit to me. If I hadn't pushed my knife in behind the leopard's foreleg I doubt if anything you could have done by remote control would have been much good. I suppose the Lolos think that you only used me as an instrument. But I'm going to let them see you're not the only god in camp! This afternoon we'll all go to the big pool upstream, and I'll put on a show they won't soon forget."

"What are you going to do?"

"Never mind. You'll find out when the time comes. Latunga can walk that far. He ought to see this, too."

After luncheon Jack asked the Lolo chief, "Do you like fish?"

"Yes, but it is difficult to catch them."

"Would you like to have many fish that you can take back to your village?"

"Of course."

"All right. Make four baskets, and I'll fill them for you."

The Lolo smiled doubtfully, but sent his men to collect vines.

Jack busied himself in the tent. He came out with a cloth-covered package and a long net over his arm. Everyone in camp followed him to the big pool a quarter of a mile above the tents. Ching, the little cook, wore a suspiciously smug expression.

The pool spread out in a circular basin fifty feet across and four or five feet in depth, between high rock walls. Hanging vines clothed the sides in a smother of green. Hundreds of fish darted about or lay quietly on the bottom.

Benton told his audience to stand on the bank; he would bring more fish to them than they had seen in all their lives. The Lolos were breathless in suspense. Even Latunga stood wide-eyed and incredulous. Jack built a tiny altar of stones and laid his covered package upon it. Then he lighted seven sticks of incense. Waving his hands above the altar, he chanted, "*Abacadabra, abacadabra, abacadabra.*" After whisking the cloth off his package, he touched a fuse at the end of a thick red cylinder to a burning incense stick. A shower of sparks flew out. Then, after waiting until the fuse had burned almost to the top of the cylinder, he tossed it into the pool. Instantly a deafening explosion sent a cone of water thirty feet into the air. The Lolos screamed and dashed into the forest. Latunga clung to Ken, trembling with fright. Ching, the cook, could hardly contain his glee. His cannon crackers had done it again!

As the echoes died in dull mutterings down the valley, scores of dead fish began drifting to the surface. Most were small, only seven or eight inches long, but some would weigh a pound or more. A dozen species were represented.

When the Lolos ventured back, Jack waved his hand. "There are the fish I promised you. Fill your baskets." They looked at him with reverence, but their eyes continually turned toward Ken. Evidently they believed that what had happened really was the Young God's doing.

Jack was amused. "It's just no use. You are the One and Only. Whatever I do stems directly from you. Well, it's all right with me. But you must admit that as your proxy I put on a pretty good show."

"You certainly did. I never would have thought of it."

"It's the way all collectors get fish, only they use dynamite. It isn't sporting, but it does produce results. Practically everything is killed by the concussion. Many species could never be taken in nets."

The Lolos waded into the pool. With Benton's net they gathered more fish than the baskets could hold. In camp Jack spread them on a tarpaulin and selected a series of each species. The cook took what he wanted for eating. The rest went to the Lolos. Two of them started back to their village, carrying full baskets slung on the ends of poles.

"Your stock is rising every day, Ken. When the women see this donation they won't believe their eyes. They've never had so much food at one time or so much excitement. As a god you are really producing the goods. Let's get to work on these fish."

The Lolo chief watched with intense interest while Jack made a solution of formalin and water. He showed Ken how to inject the fish with a long-needle syringe.

"They'll stay in the big container for a few days. When they're well preserved we'll wrap each one in cheesecloth and pack them like sardines in those flat cans with pressure tops.

They'll need only a little formalin then. Reptiles are treated just like fish."

"By the way, Jack, I've seen only two or three snakes since we came. I expected there'd be a lot of them in this valley because it's so warm and moist."

"Probably there are many, but the vegetation is so thick we just don't see them. You've given me an idea. We can capitalize on your divinity. Whenever I've been collecting near villages in other parts of China, I've used the natives to get snakes and frogs and lizards and toads. I'd tell the children that I'd pay three coppers for every one they brought. At first they wouldn't believe it. Why should anyone be fool enough to pay good money for a snake or a lizard that he couldn't eat? But after a while they'd get curious. Someone would catch a frog, and the whole village would gather around my tent while he presented it to me. When he was promptly paid, that put a different aspect on the matter. I might be crazy—probably I was—but at least I had money. If I wanted to waste it in buying snakes and frogs, that was my business. In a couple of days I'd have a good series of every species in the neighborhood.

"My thought is that we can tell the chief you'd like the children of his village to hunt those things for us. I'll bet he'll put them to work in no time."

Jack called Latunga. "Please inform the chief that the Young God wants snakes and toads and lizards and frogs. He uses them to make medicine just as he is doing with these fish. Ask him if he will have the children of his village catch such things and bring them to us. That will please the Young God greatly."

Latunga spoke rapidly to the Lolo. His face lighted. "For the Young God every man, woman, and child of my village will hunt those things. In the forest, when we turn a stone or a fallen log, they crawl away. My people will catch them and bring them here. But a few are dangerous. Do you want those also?"

"Yes we do, but you must be careful."

"The small ones we can handle with a crotched stick. But there is one great snake in this valley that we see not often. He is much longer than my body and has a wide flat head with a black mark like a hook. His bite means certain death. Two of my men have been killed by one of his kind. They died in great agony. That evil thing we dare not touch."

When Latunga translated Benton said, "Good Lord, that's a king cobra. I never thought they'd be so far north. But of course this is a tropical valley. I suppose they've made their way up from the southern jungle. It isn't very far. I'm glad to know the snake is here. It's interesting zoologically and something to look out for. If you see one, Ken, don't take any chances. Kill it but stay well away. You're a dead duck if it gets its fangs into you."

"Is its poison worse than that of other snakes?"

"No, that isn't the point. Probably the Russell's viper of India and the green mamba of Africa are deadlier so far as poison is concerned. But the king cobra is a much larger snake. I think the record is eighteen feet, four inches—that one was killed in Siam. Because it's so big the poison sacs contain a good deal more venom. Also, other snakes strike quickly and inject their venom in the fraction of a second. When the king cobra strikes it holds its victim fast until it has at least half emptied its poison sacs. There is little chance that anyone will survive a cobra bite.

"They take a terrible toll of human life, and kill a lot of animals too. I remember seeing a big water buffalo that was bitten by only a six-foot cobra. It died in a few hours, and it was a strong, young animal. A cobra has no fear of man and will attack without provocation. If you get too close to it, it'll raise two or three feet of its body off the ground, spread its hood, and go for you."

"I've read that in India the mongoose kills cobras. Are they immune to the poison?"

"No, the cobra's poison would kill a mongoose just as quickly as any other animal. But they are very agile and don't get hit. The cobra is comparatively slow in striking. The mongoose dances about in front of it and dodges when the snake strikes. After a while the cobra gets tired. Then the mongoose dashes in from behind and bites through its skull or neck.

"In Central and South America there is a very deadly and vicious snake called the fer-de-lance. It killed so many people that mongooses were introduced with the idea that they would clean out the snakes. But it didn't work. The fer-de-lance strikes like lightning and in a very short time killed all the mongooses.

"There is a kind of horrible glamour about the king cobra that no other snake possesses. In upper Burma, not very far from where we are now, some of the natives worship cobras. They believe that the snakes are responsible for good crops and many children. They even have a ceremony in which a young girl, specially trained for it, lets a cobra strike at her face time after time until it's tired out. She knows how to move her head slightly so the snake's head and neck go over her shoulder and it never really hits her. But the whole village watches and thinks it does. They think she's immune to the poison."

"What a gruesome idea!" said Ken, with a shudder. "Personally, I hate snakes. I suppose it comes from the time when I was nine years old. Dad and I were duck-shooting. The blind was built on shore about an old stump. We got there very early and had to wait quite a while for daylight. I rested my head against the stump and went to sleep. Suddenly I felt something on my neck and put up my hand. A snake coiled about my wrist. It was awful. I yelled and jumped out of the blind. Dad pulled off the snake. It was only a garter snake, but it scared me just as much as though it had been a rattler. I've never forgotten how it felt. As a matter of fact, I haven't touched a snake since that day."

"Well, I don't like them either, but I've had to collect a good many for the museum. Every time I inject one it makes me shiver, but it has to be done. I generally get a camp boy to do it under my direction. The Chinese don't seem to mind."

"What will the Lolos do with the snakes they get?" Ken asked.

"Oh, I have a lot of canvas bags of different sizes, with drawstrings. They were specially made for snake- and amphibian-collecting. I'll get them out."

Latunga gave the bags to the chief, and he started for his village at once.

"I have a strong hunch," Jack said, "that we are going to be swamped with snakes and toads, etcetera, before many hours have passed. The Young God has spoken, and, believe me, that's a divine command. Look out, snakes, here they come!"

Benton was right. Late in the evening of the next day two Lolos arrived with four wicker baskets on the ends of carrying poles, filled with squirming canvas bags. From some of them came the muffled croaking of frogs.

Benton remarked, "From what I see, this is going to be an all-day job. We'll wait until tomorrow before we open the presents."

Even though they started immediately after breakfast, it

was four o'clock in the afternoon before the haul was prepared. Every snake, lizard, toad, frog, and salamander had to
be injected and labeled, and its data recorded in the field
catalogue. The Lolos had done a thorough job in the first lot,
and when the second consignment arrived Benton found few
species new to their collection.

"This," he said to Ken, "is the pay-off for your fancy
shooting and the raw animal hearts you've eaten. I think it's
time to call off the Lolos. We have about everything they
could find near their village. After all, these collections are
just gravy for the fish and reptile departments of the museum.
They didn't contribute a cent to this expedition. All of it
comes from the Department of Mammalogy. But enough is
enough. We'll get back to our mammals. They'll keep us
busy."

"What about insects, Jack? Aren't you going to collect
any?"

"No. There are too many species, and we haven't the time.
I've already picked up a few ants for Professor Wheeler, but
that's all. By the way, there's an ant in this valley that's a
buster—more than an inch long. He's bothered me quite a
bit with the small mammal traps. I found a number of them
sprung with the bait gone and couldn't figure out what was
doing it. Then one morning I happened along as five or six of
these big ants were pulling at the pedal of a mousetrap. It was
set very lightly, of course, and as I watched, off it went. The
ants finished the peanut butter in two minutes. Then they
left. There were more ants on the next trap. It was just as
though they were following the line by the cotton markers."

"You said we were to get back on the mammals, Jack.
Where do I hunt next?"

"Latunga says the chief has told him of a swamp in the

lowest part of the valley, about a day's march from here. He says wild boar live there. We ought to get two or three of them. I'd like a family group—male, female, and young—if it is possible. I haven't finished trapping here, and there's a lot of this end of the valley that we haven't seen, so I don't want to move camp yet. I suggest that you, Latunga, and the Lolos make a trip to the swamp and see if you can get some of the pigs. How about it?"

"I'd love it, Jack, and there's something else I'd particularly like to do. I've hunted with these natives quite a lot now, and I want to see if I can live as they do and how I'd like it. We have our own food here and sleeping bags and a tent and servants. It's all very comfortable. Of course it has to be that way if we are to get any work done. But just for fun I'd like to go primitive. They eat only buttered tea, *tsampa*, and dried meat. They have no tent or sleeping bags. I'll borrow one of their felt capes and eat and sleep and live with them. I'm curious to see if I can not only endure it, but enjoy it too. The only concession to civilization will be to use my own guns and revolver. What do you say?"

Jack laughed. "Our minds certainly do run in the same groove, Ken. Years ago, on my first trip in Manchuria with Alex Chapin, I had the same idea. I did it, and loved it. For two weeks I left camp and lived with three Manchu hunters exactly as they lived—wore the same clothes, ate the same food, and slept in the open. I never had a more wonderful experience. It gave me great self-confidence. Even though I was born in a city, civilization hadn't made me soft, in either mind or body. I was just as good a man as those natives who had lived all their lives in the wilderness. I'm all for it. I predict that you'll love every minute of it."

Jack called Latunga and told him what Ken wanted to do.

The Moso was delighted. His arm was healing rapidly, and it always made him happy to be with Ken. Latunga had learned some English, and by this time Ken's Chinese was surprisingly good, for he had been studying hard. They would have no language difficulties. Ken was even beginning to understand a little of the chief's strange dialect.

Three days later they started, shortly after daylight. Ken carried a skin sack of *tsampa*, a chunk of brick tea, and a strip of dried and smoked wapiti meat; also an eating bowl. These things he packed on his back in a Lolo brown felt cape. Jack, Wu, and the cook waved good-by to them.

"Wish I were going with you," Benton said. "You'll have fun. I'll expect you back when you get here. Bring us some pig meat. The young ones are wonderful eating."

For four hours the men traveled steadily through the forest. The Lolo chief walked in front, followed by the others in single file. In the half-light, beneath the interlaced branches hanging with gray moss, they seemed like silent ghosts threading their way among the great tree trunks. Ken could think only of Indians on the warpath! Never had his mind been more alert or had his body felt stronger. There was sheer joy in every movement.

The sun was almost overhead when they reached a tiny stream in an open glade. The chief threw off his pack. "We will eat here and rest for a while," Latunga said. "The place where we sleep tonight is not far away. Near it is a pond in thick jungle. Animals often come to drink. After dark we will watch there."

One of the Lolos made a fire and boiled tea in a small iron pot. Each man filled his food bowl, put in a handful of *tsampa*, and kneaded it to a thick paste. This, with a strip of dried and smoked deer meat, was their meal.

Ken was hungry, and he devoured every scrap of food. Nothing, he thought, had ever tasted better. He lay back against a rock and smoked his pipe, utterly content. No one talked. Somehow the sound of human voices did not fit the silence and the mystery of the enclosing forest. One by one the natives finished their pipes and stretched out for a midday rest.

Ken lay down near Latunga, ten feet from the chief. He had drifted into a delightful realm of half-sleep when a sound like the soft rustling of dry leaves gradually cut through his blurred consciousness. His eyes opened to an utterly horrible, paralyzing sight. A long gray form was slowly moving up the body of the young chief. It slithered along his back and over his shoulder. A flickering tongue explored his cheek. Ken saw the Lolo's eyes open and dilate with terror as they looked into the evil face of a great king cobra. Not a muscle of the man's body moved. It was almost superhuman self-control. Only his eyes implored help from the Young God. Ken realized that at the slightest movement the serpent would strike. Slowly he stretched out his hand to the gun belt lying at his side. With infinite care he drew the revolver from its holster. The great snake's head lay flat on the chief's temple, while its red tongue ran like a devil's finger through the man's hair. Sideways, it made a very thin mark. But life, or a certain horrible death for a friend, was the stake. Ken fired like a flash.

At the roar of his gun the cobra's head disintegrated in a splatter of bloody bits. On the instant the chief rolled to the left and leaped away. The reptile's body writhed in twisting folds over the spot where the Lolo had been lying.

The shot brought every man to his feet. None of them realized what had happened. Ken was sitting, shaking, when the chief knelt in front of him. The man's face was gray-white.

He tried to speak, but no words came through his dry lips. Putting his two hands together, he touched them to his forehead and bowed to the ground. In his eyes shone a light of infinite gratitude.

Ken sensed that it was not because the Lolo feared death that he was so affected. In his code, death was to be expected. If it came from a spear thrust or a bullet or an arrow, he could look it in the face and laugh. But that a loathsome reptile should stare into his eyes while it poured its deadly poison into his flesh was not an honorable death for a Lolo chieftain. The Young God had saved more than his life.

Ken had difficulty in gaining control of his nerves. Never before had he fired a bullet where the chance was so close between the life and death of a human being. It had been quite different with the bandits on the hilltop. There he had been attacked. During exhibition shoots near New York, his competitors had sometimes shot cigarettes from the mouths of spectators or done the William Tell act of knocking an apple off the head of a man. Ken would have none of these performances. It was not the size of the mark that disturbed him—that was simple. He always carried the thought that a human being is not a machine. His body and brain and eyes are susceptible to unaccountable and uncertain changes. One could never be sure that some strange reaction might not send the bullet into the head of a trusting person. To him that would be murder, whether or not the law considered it to be so.

When he saw the cobra lying on the body of the chief, there had been no time to think. At any moment the snake might strike. He had the power to kill the reptile. The decision was not in his hands. He could only thank God that an unusual talent gave him that power.

Even though its head had been smashed to bits, the cobra's body was still writhing in the throes of involuntary muscle action. When at last it was still the Lolos stretched it out and paced its length. Nearly twelve feet—one of the largest of its kind!

Neither Ken nor the chief could bring himself to touch it, but Latunga and the other Lolos skinned the reptile. Its stomach was empty. Evidently it had been on the prowl for a meal. The skin was hung to dry on a vine between two trees. It would be picked up on their return.

Two hours before dark the men dropped their packs beside a small pool. Animal tracks showed in the mud, but the Lolos said there was a much larger pond not far off.

Just at dusk Latunga, Ken, and the chief made their way through the forest to a lakelet in a small open meadow. They settled themselves in a clump of bushes near the water's edge. In half an hour the velvety blackness of a tropic night enveloped them like a cloak. Then the moon pushed a brilliant edge over the treetops, flooding the water with silver light. They sat motionless, listening to the breath of the jungle. Now and then a muntjac barked hoarsely, and the roar of a stag thrilled Ken like an electric shock. Once a wild boar grunted, the sound coming clear and sharp through the stillness. A leopard coughed on the opposite side of the pond. Ken felt Latunga stir beside him and push his gun forward. He was thinking of his mangled arm, still only half healed. Tiny forest creatures rustled in the grass. Once a mouse ran across Ken's lap, leaping frantically into the bushes as he moved.

For five hours they waited, but no animals came to drink at the pond. Probably the man-scent on the air drifted across the water, although there was no wind. But as they groped their way back to camp Ken felt a great happiness. He had been close to the heart of the jungle and was thrilled with the mystery of the night.

The Lolos left at the pool had collected a great pile of wood. A huge fire sent long shafts of light into the forest. After eating, the men wrapped themselves in their capes and stretched out on the ground. "No fear of snakes or leopards," Latunga said. "We'll keep the fire burning through the night."

With his knife Ken dug a shallow trench for his hip and shoulder. In five minutes he was asleep.

By ten o'clock next morning they stood at the edge of a great marsh, or rather a series of marshes. Low areas filled with tall grass, but not very wet, were separated by higher ground like islands rising out of a waving brown sea. This, said Latunga, was where the wild boars lived and reared their young. He and Ken would take stations on the ridges, while the Lolos walked through the grass toward them. Ken had given Latunga his 12-gauge shotgun and shells loaded with lead balls. They were deadly at short range, and the Moso was a good shot. Ken had his 9-mm. Mannlicher.

He and Latunga worked through the waist-high grass to a ridge, only slightly above the marsh floor. When the Lolo chief saw they were in position, he and his three men moved toward them, shouting and pounding sticks together.

The guns had only a few minutes to wait. Ken saw the high grass parting like the line of a fish swimming at the surface in shallow water. The waving path moved directly toward him. Suddenly, out of a tiny open space, burst a huge brown boar, his little eyes red with rage and his jaws chopping over foam-flecked lips. Ken fired quickly. The pig went down but struggled to its feet and charged again. The second bullet dropped him at six feet from the rifle's end. Latunga's gun boomed at the left—two shots; then two more; and a final one. Ken looked at the Moso. He was doing a war dance, hopping up and down, holding the gun above his head and screaming at the top of his voice. Obviously he had scored; how many, Ken had no idea.

After making sure that the big boar was dead, he walked over to Latunga. Three pigs lay in front of him, the nearest at the bottom of the rise. One was a big sow, the other two half-grown piglets. While the boar drove at Ken, the young had followed their mother in hopes of escape. Jack's group had been completed in the first drive.

The chief and the other Lolos pulled the pigs to dry ground. There Ken measured them, and the natives took over the skinning job. Latunga and he had to eat their bits of heart from each animal in the hunting ceremony. By now that had become a habit to Ken. He minded it not at all.

The skins and skulls of all four animals, and the meat of the young porkers plus the sow, made heavy loads for the men. Ken judged his weighed seventy pounds, but he was determined not to carry less than the natives. They respected his wishes, and his pack was a little heavier than any of the others. When they reached the main camp two days later, Ken was happy. He knew he could take it as well as any native.

XVI. In Lolo Land

FOR a month the expedition remained in the Valley of the Flowers, moving from place to place. At every camp new and interesting specimens were collected, but spring had given place to summer. The days were uncomfortably hot, and rains soaked the jungle almost every night. After a conference with Latunga and the Lolo chief, Benton said to Ken, "It's time for us to go north. Even on the high mountains it will be getting warm. The chief has made a suggestion that I think is splendid. He is very grateful to you, and he wants to do something for us. He says that in northern Lolo Land, on the frontier of Tibet, there are very high mountains. He has never been there, but he feels sure we would find snow leopard. Latunga thinks so too.

"No white man has ever seen that part of Lolo Land. The chief would go with us and be our sponsor. With him we'd be passed from one village to another. He says we would be perfectly safe. Latunga thinks that region would be somewhat nearer than the place where he got the two snow leopards last year. I'm all for it. What do you say?"

Ken was thrilled. "It would be a wonderful opportunity. We'd learn more about the Lolos than anyone has ever known. I wonder how much their bad reputation is deserved. Probably it stems from the Chinese. The Lolos want to keep people out of their country just as the Tibetans do. It's their privilege, if they can. If the Lolos in the village here are fair examples, they're darned nice people. As a whole I like them better than any other Orientals we've met."

"I agree with you. Their situation is exactly like that of our American Indians. The Lolos originally were in possession of much of western China. They were driven out by the Chinese, just as white men drove our Indians from their homelands. The only difference is that the Lolos were able to keep possession of a big area in western Szechuan. It's so rugged and mountainous that the Chinese can't do much about it. But it just burns them up. They hate the Lolos, just as many white men hated the Indians."

The next day Benton and Ken spread out all their trays of small mammals and birds in the sun; also the big skins were given a careful inspection. This was the final drying before the boxes and bales were tied up in oiled silk and canvas. Moreover, the fish, reptiles, and amphibians had to be taken from the large containers. Each one had to be wrapped separately in cheesecloth and packed like sardines in pressure-top tins. These were sealed with paraffin.

Ken was amazed at the number of specimens. They had collected nearly two thousand mammals and five hundred birds, to say nothing of several hundred fish and reptiles.

Benton looked at them with enormous satisfaction. "This," he said, "is the biggest collection ever taken out of southwestern China. And most of it is from a region that no naturalist has visited. It is just about worth its weight in gold to a museum. I wouldn't dare guess how many species will be new to science. Already the trip is a great success, even if we don't make up another specimen. We won't get very many more either, because we'll be traveling pretty constantly.

"If we can capture a snow leopard, that will be the climax. I think we will, too. You may be sure that if there is one in Lolo Land, the chief will have it for us. What a fortunate thing it was that we dropped into their village, and that your shooting put you in the class of a major divinity! Ever since you shot that cobra off the chief's face he looks at you with absolute adoration."

Ken smiled. "Things have worked out pretty well. But I hope I'll not have to do any more stunts like that to keep my reputation. It's too hard on my nerves. As long as I live I'll have a mind-picture of that horrible thing lying on his body with the tongue flicking out over his face. I still dream about it."

Two mornings later, as the caravan climbed the steep trail, Benton turned back for a last look over the vast green sea of gently waving treetops. "Good-by, valley," he said. "You don't owe us anything."

The chief had already gone to the village, and when they arrived a feast had been prepared at the ceremonial amphitheater. Every man, woman, and child of the community was there to do them honor.

Next day the chief guided them to one of the great trade routes into Tibet. Over it caravans were continually passing, loaded with brick tea and salted pork. Some of them had traveled the entire length of Yunnan to S'su-mao on the Tonking frontier, where a special kind of tea was grown, and were on the way back.

They camped the second night at an altitude of 10,000 feet, in a beautiful forest near the road. Damp bamboo stalks made a brilliant and noisy fire. As the hollow stems filled with steam they exploded like firecrackers. "If I'm not mistaken," Jack remarked, "Marco Polo recorded this same phenomenon in just this area. I'm going to look it up." Sure enough, there it was in the Venetian traveler's book, written more than six centuries ago!

A big caravan stopped very near their tents. Ken visited it with the chief. The Tibetans were picturesque, wild-looking fellows. They all wore fur caps and long, loose coats thrown carelessly off one shoulder and tied about the waist. Blue or red trousers and knee-high boots of felt or skin completed their costumes. None was without a long sword, its hilt inlaid with bits of bright-colored glass or stones. Several were also armed with a cheek gun or a murderous-looking spear.

In the breast of his loose coat, which acted as a pocket, each one carried an assortment of necessary things—a pipe, tobacco, tea, *tsampa*, a cooking pot, and a snuffbox. Hanging down in front was a metal charm to protect the man from bullets or sickness.

Some were men of splendid physique, more than six feet tall. They had brick-red complexions and were really handsome in a full-blooded, masculine way. In their strength and virility and the dashing swing of the walk, one felt the atmosphere of the bleak Tibetan steppes where they made their homes.

Jack read to Ken what Major Davies had to say in his book about the Yunnan Tibetans. He remarked how little impression the civilization and customs of the Chinese have produced on the Tibetans. Elsewhere the power of the Chinese in absorbing other races is amazing. But with the Tibetans exactly the opposite takes place. The Chinese become "Tibetanized," and the children of a Chinese married to a Tibetan woman are usually brought up in the Tibetan customs.

Probably, Major Davies says, the great factor that keeps the Tibetans from being absorbed is the cold, inhospitable nature of their country. There is little to tempt the Chinese to emigrate into Tibet, and consequently they never are there in sufficient numbers to influence the Tibetans around them.

For nine days the expedition traveled the road toward Tibet; then the Lolo chief turned abruptly eastward on a little-used trail. Villages became smaller and widely scattered. They crossed the border into Szechuan Province, and from the summit of a pass saw three Lolo houses halfway down the slope. The chief halted the caravan while he went forward alone. After half an hour he returned with a tall, pleasant-faced Lolo. He gave the Tibetan greeting of protruding his tongue, with an additional accessory of scratching his right ear. Jack and Ken stuck out their tongues and scratched their ears, managing with difficulty to keep from laughing.

The man said there was a large and important settlement of Lolos at a place called Habala not far to the east. They must be informed and permission obtained from them before the expedition could proceed with safety. He suggested that the expedition camp while he and the young chief and Latunga went on to the village. Benton agreed, of course, and the tents were pitched on a level terrace near the houses.

By mid-afternoon the men returned with two other Lolos, After tongue-protruding and ear-scratching, Latunga introduced them as the chief of Habala and his brother. They had come, he said, to inspect the caravan. Jack gave them tea and cigarettes. The Lolos seemed friendly and frankly curious. Never before, they admitted, had they seen people like these. As usual the blue and gray eyes created the most interest. Both Jack and Ken were deeply tanned, but they opened their shirts to show their white skins. The Lolos were astounded. They suggested that next morning the caravan should come to Habala. There further conference with the elders would take place.

Not long after daylight the caravan was on the move. The trail led down the mountain into a beautiful valley. About sixty houses made a picturesque group on the level floor. Small fields of barley were showing fresh green shoots in the warm spring sunshine. Two or three flocks of goats, tended by young boys in brown felt capes, grazed on a knoll. But most interesting to Ken were a dozen great, black, shaggy animals. They looked more like Arctic musk oxen than anything else.

"What are they, Jack?"

"Those are yaks. You'll be riding one before long, I hope. The Tibetans use them almost entirely on the high mountain slopes. They can go anywhere and live on moss and alpine vegetation where other animals would starve. These are domesticated from wild yaks. They furnish milk and butter and cheese and good meat."

A few hundred yards from Habala their friends of the day before met them and directed the caravan to a flat green lawn.

The proceedings were much like those at their first Lolo village. Delegations of men and boys arrived. All were curious, but not offensively so. Eventually many women came. Jack distributed the last of his steel mirrors with much effect. The women and girls were most excited by Ken's white skin, and very envious. One of them asked if he had to take many baths to keep as white as that!

Latunga and the chief had publicized Ken's shooting, and the village elders asked if he would give them an exhibition. They could not believe, they said, that such things were possible. They must see it with their own eyes.

Everyone in the village gathered in front of the camp. There were more than two hundred men, women, and children. Jack said, "You never had a more important audience, even when you shot in New York at Madison Square Garden. If you make as great an impression as you did before, we can have anything we want in Lolo Land."

This time the young Lolo chief acted as master of ceremonies, and he outdid even Latunga. Ken fired with the Mannlicher at smaller and smaller pieces of wood. The chief tossed blocks for him, and he broke three, and finally four, before they touched the ground. He seemed inspired as he drew and shot with his revolver. Afterward he said, "I've never been able to do it that well before. Probably I can never reach such speed again."

At first the audience exclaimed in amazement. Then they paid him the great compliment of stunned silence. At last the young chief clapped his hands. He walked to the center of the circle and began to talk. Latunga translated for Jack and Ken. With the drama of a natural actor, the Lolo told how Ken had saved his life when a great cobra crawled over his body; how he had lain, frozen with terror, as the cold, flat head moved across his face, the tongue flicking over his skin; how he had seen the Young God wake, stretch out his hand, and slowly, very slowly, draw his revolver—then, like a flash of light, fire at the hideous thing that lay upon the chief's temple. He described how the reptile's head flew into a dozen pieces and how he had rolled away. No one but the Young God could have saved him from a horrible and humiliating death.

Then the Lolo related what the expedition had done for his people. He acted brilliantly the death of the two *ma lou* as they dashed out of the forest glade—how the great stag had turned a somersault, burying its antlers in the earth when the Young God's bullet struck. And two seconds later the other lay dead with a broken neck! His village, he said, had had great feasts on the meat. He told of the fish that had given them more food than ever before. Then he spoke with passionate intensity. "These men are my friends and friends of my people. They wish to travel in Lolo Land to take out, alive, a snow leopard. I ask that they be given permission to go where they wish and to receive help from every Lolo, no matter where he lives. This is a sacred obligation placed upon us by the Gods of the Hunt, who have sent one of their number to show us favor."

It was a masterly speech, with perfect timing. When the young chief stepped away a murmur of approbation ran through the crowd like a breeze stirring the leaves of an aspen tree. The head man of the settlement walked to the center of the circle. He bowed to Ken and Jack and to the young chief. With grave courtesy he thanked them for what the people had seen and heard that afternoon.

"Tonight," he said, "I will confer with others who are wise, in council. No strangers have ever been allowed in Lolo Land.

But," he remarked with a smile, "there must always be a first time."

That night Ken and Latunga smoked a pipe with the young chief around the fire. Ken thanked him for what he had done. The Lolo answered, "I know my people. You need not fear. They will give us what we have asked."

Next morning five of the Habala elders visited the camp. A vote had been taken, they said, and all agreed that permission should be given the strangers to travel in Lolo Land. Moreover, they had conferred with the village hunters. Several of them said they knew snow leopards were to be found on the high mountains to the east and north, but that they were rare. The elders suggested that the expedition remain at Habala until the hunters had located an animal. This would save them much effort.

Jack was delighted. They would have time not only to do some collecting but to learn more of Lolo life and customs from the people of this community.

A week later the first hunter returned; two others came back within a few hours. Two of them reported success. They had gone to three different areas, and people from small villages high up on the mountains said snow leopards were there. They lived on the gray monkeys, on young yaks and goats. A very big leopard near a village called Kulu had killed two herdboys and eaten one. Those Lolos would be particularly happy if the strangers rid them of the beast.

Benton decided to leave the mules and part of the equipment at Habala. They could hire yaks from the villagers to carry what they needed for a small camp high up in the mountains. Two of the Lolo hunters would go with them.

Ken found riding a yak to be an amusing experience. His regular McClellan saddle was strapped on the great shaggy beast, but his feet almost touched the ground. The yak didn't like either Ken or the saddle and grunted continually just like a pig. Eventually it became resigned, but Ken felt he was only being tolerated as a necessary evil; he and the yak would never be real friends.

For two days the little caravan plodded steadily along rocky trails toward a snow-capped mountain. Mile by mile the land rose, until they were at an altitude of 14,000 feet. Then it leveled off for half a day's march on the broad summit of a wooded ridge. There they found six Lolo houses, a few yaks, and a herd of goats. This was Kulu, where the snow leopard had killed the two herdboys.

The Lolos were happy to see them. They pointed to a steep grassy slope covered with a jumble of rocks and boulders, three thousand feet above the village. There, they said, was where the snow leopard lived. It had been on the mountain for some time, they knew, but only last winter had it caused them trouble. Perhaps it was because of unusually heavy snow, but anyway the animal had often come near their village. One day while two of the boys were watching goats, they had almost stepped on the great cat asleep behind a rock. It killed both boys. One of them it pulled away and ate before the villagers could find the body.

The Habala hunters suggested that the expedition go up the mountain at once and camp just within the growth of dwarf bamboo that reached right to the edge of the rocky slope. With them Jack and Ken were to take a very young yak. It could be purchased from the Kulu villagers for ten silver dollars. The yak would be better than a goat, even though it was more expensive, because goats seldom went up there, whereas yaks often did. Thus the snow leopard would not be suspicious.

The yak would be staked out and left at night. Eventually the leopard would find and kill it. But it could not be eaten at one sitting. So the traps which the strangers had shown the Kulu hunters could be set about the carcass. The leopard would certainly return to finish the yak and, of course, be caught. It was as simple as that.

Benton could find no flaws in the plan. With one of the Kulu Lolos as a guide, the yaks worked their way up a trail almost as steep as the side of a house, to a small level open meadow thickly carpeted with brown grass, in the bamboo jungle. There the Lolos pitched a tiny silk tent big enough only for two sleeping bags. For themselves they built a skeleton shelter of dwarf-bamboo poles, and covered it with long dry grass. Above them the bamboo petered out in a ragged edge of whiplike stalks to the open mountainside covered with a chaos of great boulders. Patches of snow lay among the rocks, and farther up, a solid stretch of gleaming white spread over the crest and away into the peaks and chasms of far-off mountains—a wild, lonely place, fit home for one of the strangest animals in all the world.

After camp was made, the Lolos took the young yak to a spot among the rocks where many bones were lying. A hundred yards away the mouth of a cave showed black against the snow. "That," said the Kulu guide, "is where the leopard lives."

The yak was tethered firmly to a rock, where it could graze on the long grass. But it wasn't happy. As the men made their way down the slope, its blatting sounded like an accusing voice through the stillness of the mountain night.

XVII. End of the Quest

NEXT morning Jack and Ken went with the Lolos to the young yak. It was quietly grazing at the end of its rope. The snow leopard had not been near it. One of the hunters gathered a quantity of sand and scattered it at the door of the cave. If the leopard went either in or out it would leave tracks. They took the little yak back to camp. It would be tethered again at dusk.

Jack got out six wolf traps he had brought from New York. "Ken, please find that roll of black tire tape in the small duffel sack," he said, "and we'll fix these traps."

Each jaw was heavily wound with tape. This made enough

of a cushion to keep the steel from cutting into the animal's leg.

"What is your plan?" Ken asked.

"After the yak has been killed we'll set all the traps about the carcass. The leopard is sure to return, and it can't help but get into at least one, and probably two traps. The drags will keep it from going far or injuring itself in pulling. I can throw a rope fairly well, and we'll lasso it and tie it up—then release the traps and put it into a cage which Latunga and the chief will make today out of bamboo. They'll fasten the cage to poles so it can swing between two yaks or mules. Then we'll start for Yünnanfu and the railroad by the shortest route. That's the program. What do you think of it?"

"Sounds all right to me. The only trouble is that then the expedition will be ended and we'll have to say good-by to Latunga and the chief. I don't want to think of it. I suppose we'll never see them again."

"Probably not, but you can't tell. It's possible our collections will show things that will make it necessary to come back for more material. But, Ken, you'll often have to say good-by to men who work with you. You get awfully fond of some of them, and it is difficult. But Latunga will always stand out as the finest one I've ever known. And I have a very real affection for the chief too. He certainly has done a lot for us. Let's get them started on the cage. It'll take a little time, for it must be strong."

Jack explained what he wanted to Latunga. The cage was to be six feet long, three feet high, and three feet wide, with a door at the top. The bars must be so close together that the leopard could not get his paws between them.

Not only Latunga and the chief, but all the other Lolos, set to work at once, collecting three-inch stalks of green bamboo

and tough, pliable vines. They kept at it all day, and by dark
the job was done. It was an amazingly good piece of work.
The ends of the bamboo were notched and fitted and bound
with vines stronger than leather thongs.

Jack examined it with much satisfaction. "This," he said,
"could go around the world without breaking. It's infinitely
better than boards and nails, particularly for carrying between
mules. The bamboo and vines make it wonderfully elastic. I
hope we'll have the snow leopard to put in it soon."

But it was more than a week before they had action. Every
morning one or two of the men inspected the little yak. It
grunted disconsolately but seemed to have become resigned
to the lonely nights on the mountain. At the entrance to the
cave the sand remained unmarked. The leopard was prowling
somewhere in the far peaks or snow-filled valleys to the north.

Ken and Jack were not impatient. They had a line of fifty
or sixty small traps and reaped a harvest of mammals. The high
altitude, combined with the bare, rocky slopes and bamboo
jungle, gave a completely new fauna. All day they worked at
making up skins, much to the Lolos' interest. Ken couldn't
hunt, for they didn't want to fire a gun anywhere in the
vicinity of the snow leopard's home. Latunga was somewhat
disappointed, for he learned from the Lolos that a curious
mountain animal called *yeh niu* (wild cow) lived in the vicinity.

"That," said Jack, "is the takin. It's one of the *Rupicaprinæ*
but, strangely enough, is more closely related to the Arctic
musk ox than to serows or gorals. Only two or three white
men have ever killed it. We have one in the museum that was
shot by Mason Mitchell when he was American Consul at
Chungking, China. He got it near Tatsienlu, not very far
from here, in 1907. He sent a skin to the museum and one to

Rowland Ward's in London. It proved to be new species and was named in his honor, *Budorcas mitchelli.*

"There's another strange beast somewhere in these mountains. It's the giant panda. It lives in the dense bamboo jungles. The French missionary-scientist Père David discovered it fifty years ago. It's about the size of a bear and is strikingly colored. Around the eyes are black patches like spectacles. Its ears are black, and there is a heavy band of black over its shoulders and front legs. The rest of the body is white. No one knows much about it, for it has never been shot by a white man."

Ken sighed. "Gosh, I'd like to have a go at those beasts. But I suppose it can't be done."

"Not on this trip, Ken. We've got to stick to our specified job. You remember I told you how easy it is to get off into bypaths that seem too fascinating to miss. With our magnificent collection, if we can get a snow leopard, we've produced a hundred per cent. The takin and the panda will have to wait, even if they aren't far away. I'm sure that now we could come back to Lolo Land any time we wanted to."

On the morning of the eighth day the chief went up to the young yak alone and returned in great excitement. The calf had been killed, he said, and half eaten. Tracks were all over the sand at the mouth of the cave. Probably the snow leopard was inside, sleeping after its big meal.

With the traps and bamboo drags, the men hurried up the steep slope. The yak lay near where it had been tethered. Its neck was broken and one side mostly eaten. Fortunately it had been left in a place where the traps, chains, and drags could easily be buried and concealed in the long grass. The men surrounded the carcass with traps. The hunters all agreed that the leopard must surely be caught if it returned to the kill.

Jack and Ken had a restless night. Neither could sleep for a long time. They sat about the fire, talking of the expedition and future plans. The crowning achievement was so near they could hardly wait for daylight.

Benton would let no one go up the slope until full dawn, although the Lolos were impatient to be off. Ken carried his Mannlicher, and Latunga was armed with the shotgun and ball shells. Benton had a thirty-foot rope lasso.

They came through the thick wall of bamboo jungle to a breathtaking picture. Far above them the jagged peak, still bathed in dawn tints of lavender and pink, pushed out of a blanket of white clouds. Below the snowline rocks and great boulders showed black against the sky. In the foreground an incredibly beautiful animal crouched on the body of the dead yak. Lips drawn back, green eyes blazing, snarling a deadly menace, the snow leopard stood like a figure cast in silver. Even the Lolos gasped at the beauty of the picture.

The men approached slowly, Ken and Latunga in front with guns ready. But it was unnecessary caution. The leopard was held by three traps—two behind and one in front. The chains and drags were so tangled that the animal could hardly move. Jack was happy to see that the trap jaws had not cut the skin on any leg.

It was simple to throw a noose about the leopard's neck. With the Lolos hanging to the trap chains on the hind legs, Jack stretched it tight. Latunga tied the four legs with short ropes. Then he put a muzzle over the jaws and released the traps. After stringing the animal on a bamboo pole, they went carefully down the mountainside back to camp. Half an hour later the first snow leopard ever to be taken alive was in its bamboo cage.

For a time the beast raged in impotent fury. Throwing itself against the bars, it clawed and snarled. Finally it ceased fighting and lay quiet in sullen wrath. The leopard was a big male in perfect condition. Dark gray spots broke up the ground color of cream gray, shading into white on the underparts. The tail, four feet long and as large around as a man's two hands, waved like a magnificent plume. The fur looked to be as soft as a chinchilla's coat.

"If we can get this animal safely to New York it will create a sensation at the zoo. I've never seen such a spectacular creature," Jack said. "But it's going to need constant care. Coming down from seventeen thousand feet to sea level and the heat of summer will be a big change. Still, cats are hard to kill. It will have six weeks, at least, in which to get acclimated, for we couldn't possibly reach Yünnanfu sooner than that. Also the change, both in altitude and temperature, will be gradual. The veterinarian at the zoo said he felt sure it could be done."

"Will you give me the job of looking after him?" Ken asked. "I've had a lot of pet animals, and maybe I could tame him enough so he'd be easier to handle. If only one person fed and watered him and cleaned his cage, it would be a good thing. He'd get to know me and, I'm sure, would calm down. When I was working at the zoo in New York one summer I had quite a lot to do with the leopards. You can't trust them too far, and I never did, but one became quite friendly with me."

"I'd like nothing better than to have you take over, Ken. As a matter of fact, I was going to ask if you would. I'm sure you can do a lot toward taming the beast. Also some one person must have the responsibility. 'What's everyone's job is no one's job.' From now on he's your leopard."

"That's swell. Will you please ask Latunga to bring down

what's left of the yak? After a while the leopard is going to eat. He won't until he gets awfully hungry. But all leopards like their meat 'high.' The yak will be just about ripe enough by the time he makes up his mind that he can't get out and begins to relax. By the way, he's got to have a name. What'll we call him?"

"I was thinking of that. How about 'Rajah'? He's a king beast if there ever was one."

"That fits him. People back home will like it too. Do you know, it seems strange that no one has ever captured a snow leopard before this. We've done it so easily."

"Yes, now that we're here, but think of what has gone on to put us here. For one thing, snow leopards are rare, particularly in the Himalayas near India, where white men have hunted. The places where they live are all forbidden territory. In neither Tibet nor Lolo Land are foreigners welcome, as you know. Much of the country is unexplored. None of the peaks that you can see from here are named. This is just a blank space on the map.

"It's very expensive to send an expedition like this from either America or Europe, even though it might get a lot of other animals and birds. The zoo in New York couldn't afford it. When the director heard that I was coming out here he said one of their trustees would pay part of the expenses of the expedition if we could capture a snow leopard and bring it back to New York alive. That's one reason why it is so important to us.

"Last night, after we'd turned in, I couldn't sleep. I know you couldn't either. I went over in my mind the chain of events that put us here in Lolo Land. It's very interesting. First is Latunga in Lichiang with his snow-leopard skins. Then he comes up to the temple and sees our small mammals. He is enough intrigued with us and our job to go with us. Then we blunder into the Lolo village. You become a god. You shoot a cobra off the chief's face and save his life. He sponsors us for travel in Lolo Land, where no white man has ever been allowed. You impress the Habala Lolos. They send out hunters to find snow leopards. So here we are with the first one ever to be captured safely in its cage. It's an interesting story, and, I may say, you are responsible for much of its success."

"Thanks, Jack, but I wouldn't be here if it weren't for you. Don't think I forget that. I do hope we can deliver Rajah in New York safely. I have a feeling that we can."

That night Ken went out to look at the leopard. The eyes seemed to glow with green fire in the flashlight ray. He snarled and moved restlessly from side to side. The water basin fixed to the bars inside the cage was empty. Ken refilled it and for fifteen minutes talked in soothing tones to the great beast. Then he crawled into his sleeping bag, shivering with cold. The temperature was only twenty degrees above zero.

Next day Jack collected the traps and packed their specimens. Rajah was quiet but threw himself violently against the bars of the cage when anyone came near. Ken dropped half a dozen chunks of yak meat through the door just before dark. In the morning they had vanished. Several times during the day Ken sat by the cage, talking to the big cat. By evening the leopard was definitely quieter.

Latunga had made a rope sling for each end of the two poles supporting the cage. These fitted over the shoulders of the yaks. They had no difficulty in getting down the mountain to Kulu. The Lolos were delighted that the man-eater would bother them no more, and particularly so when Benton gave thirty silver dollars to the head man for their help.

Their arrival at Habala was triumphal. Jack asked the village elders to kill goats and provide a feast for the entire community at his expense. By request, Ken gave another shooting demonstration.

After a conference with the Habala head man, Jack decided that the shortest route to Yünnanfu and the railroad was across the northern part of Lolo Land to Tachow. That town was just within Chinese-controlled territory. From there they could strike directly south to the city of Ningyuan and to Yünnanfu. The head man said he would give them an escort of Lolos who would pass them from one village to the next. They left with ten Lolos two days later in an aura of friendship and good will.

The young chief and Latunga went with them. Jack had asked if they would not like to go to Yünnanfu; there they would see things they had never dreamed existed, and they could return together. Both agreed instantly. By now they were fast friends.

As the caravan traveled eastward day after day, the valleys broadened and became less rugged. They saw houses and cultivated fields. From the hillsides rose groups of Lolos, wild-looking fellows in black turbans and great brown capes. They streamed down on the caravan, waving guns, crossbows, and spears, until they saw the escort. Then they became most friendly.

As each group left and turned them over to another, Benton gave them "wine money," and they smiled and bowed their thanks. Gathered on a nearby ridge, they watched until the caravan disappeared. At the first signs of Chinese cultivation, the escort from the last Lolo village said they could go no farther without danger to themselves. It was the eastern frontier of Lolo Land, the scene of almost continuous warfare. Raid and reprisal succeeded each other in a never-ending series.

They found Tachow to be a walled town, a frontier outpost always under arms. Only that morning a village not a mile from the walls had been burned by hill Lolos, and one soldier had been killed. The magistrate was astounded when he heard where they had been. He could hardly believe that the expedition had lived for weeks in Lolo Land and crossed without robbery or trouble. He said that never had a white man been there, and that for many years no Chinese had ventured more than a few miles from the town.

Ever since leaving Habala Ken had made good progress with Rajah. Within a few days the leopard had begun to eat in the daytime as well as at night. Ken always fed him when they camped at the end of each march. At first the meat was dropped in from the door; later he put choice bits on the end of a stick and pushed it through the bars. When the meal was finished he talked to the animal in quiet tones for half an hour. Sometimes the cat would stretch out with half-closed eyes in which there was no light of fear or hate.

From a piece of bamboo Ken cut a crude likeness of a human hand with curved fingers. One day when Rajah was lying quietly, Ken attempted to scratch behind the leopard's ears. The cat struck the stick away with his paw. A few minutes later Ken tried again. After half a dozen attempts Rajah realized that this was not only nothing to fear but something pleasant. Before long Ken was able to scratch the leopard's throat while Rajah stretched out his neck and purred like a great housecat.

Ken loved animals, and in some mysterious way all animals sensed the fact. They trust to instincts that are far more reliable than a man's logical mind. The day that Rajah definitely responded to his name Ken was tremendously excited. It was a real triumph.

As they traveled southward toward Yünnanfu the crowds of curious Chinese became a serious problem. They pressed so closely about the cage that Rajah was frantic. Sometimes the caravan was almost swamped in gaping humanity. This was particularly bad near a village; on the country roads they could handle the people with less difficulty.

One day the caravan passed half a dozen coolies staggering under the weight of a heavy coffin. On it rode a fine rooster. "Why the cock?" Jack asked. Latunga explained that the deceased had died a long way from home and that his body was being carried back to be buried in the ancestral cemetery. At the time of death, his spirit was supposed to have entered the rooster and would be transported by it back to his home.

Ken heard the conversation. At the next town he bought a large square of cloth and a white rooster. He covered Rajah's cage and tied the bird on top by one leg.

"From now on," he announced, "this is the body of my uncle, which I am returning to our native city of Yünnanfu. Since I don't have an uncle it's all right to create a dead one."

Jack laughed. "By golly, I'll bet it works." And it did. When the caravan entered a town it was accorded due respect for the dead. The deceased, people assumed, must have been rich and of great importance to warrant such an imposing procession.

At last the caravan reached Yünnanfu, and they camped in a temple on the shore of the beautiful lake. Jack immediately sent Wu to find a Chinese carpenter. He and Ken designed a larger and more comfortable cage in which Rajah could move about with freedom. The leopard was in excellent condition.

He showed no ill effects from the long journey and change of climate and altitude. In the new cage he purred his thanks—at least, he purred!

Jack found that the S.S. *Haitan*, on which they had come, was due in Haiphong the following week. It would take them to Hong Kong, where they could immediately transfer to the Canadian Pacific's S.S. *Empress of Japan*. She would go via the great circle northern route to Vancouver, British Columbia. On the trip across Canada and down to New York, Rajah would escape most of the summer's heat.

At the Standard Oil Company's office they found an accumulation of seven months' mail. Ken opened the last letter from his family first, to see if they were all well. Then he arranged the rest of the letters by dates and began at the oldest and read them in chronological order.

Cables reporting the success of the expedition brought gratifying replies from the directors of the museum and Zoological Society and Ken's father and mother. The Hong Kong correspondents of world news agencies wired for interviews. Jack and Ken were swamped with invitations from the cosmopolitan community of Yünnanfu. Ken was beginning to experience the effects of the glamour that surrounds a successful explorer. He liked it.

In the meantime Latunga and the chief lived in an unbelievable world. The Lolo continued to wear his black turban and brown cape; Latunga stuck to the skin jacket, short trousers, and little skullcap that were his native costume. Their dress caused some glances of interest, but not many, for Yünnanfu was still a frontier city where natives of a dozen Oriental tribes walked the streets.

Jack and Ken never tired of taking them about town. After the first shock of amazement they seemed to move in a daze.

The peak of incredulity had been attained almost at once. Beyond that nothing could reach a higher register.

The railroad, of course, produced the most startling reaction. Ken took them to the station the day after their arrival. On the way he tried to describe what they would see, but his words must have conveyed little to their numbed brains. When the engine puffed up to the platform with clanging bells and hissing steam, both the men screamed and dashed up the street. Ken finally discovered them huddled together in a corner of the wall, shaking in utter terror.

Back at the temple, Jack explained that what seemed like a living dragon, straight from hell, breathing fire and smoke, was not alive but only a man-made thing of steel and iron. It did no good. Latunga and the chief firmly believed it to be a Chinese dragon. No words could change what their eyes had seen!

Benton sold their mules and paid off the men. Of the equipment he asked Latunga and the chief to select what they wanted. They wished for nothing except a few steel traps, some knives, and two pairs of field glasses. The remaining things Jack disposed of to Chinese traders in the bazaar.

Both he and Ken loved their Mannlicher rifles, but to Latunga and the chief they would be of inestimable value. As Jack said, "Without either of those men the expedition couldn't have produced such wonderful results. Besides that, Latunga saved my life. We can get other rifles; they can't. I'd like to give mine."

Ken agreed enthusiastically. So they asked the two men to come into the temple, where they sat on their camp beds below a grinning idol. Jack thanked them for what they had done, and he and Ken presented them with the rifles and three hundred rounds of ammunition for each.

Latunga and the chief could only gasp in unbelieving joy. In their wildest dreams they had never expected such a thing could happen to them. As return gifts Latunga brought his crossbow, arrows in a bear's-paw quiver, and a box of poison; the chief produced his long-barreled gun and its coil of fuse rope. These were their most valued possessions. With simple dignity they asked Jack and Ken to accept their offerings.

The time for parting came early one morning when the mist was curling in white spirals over the surface of the lake. The baggage and Rajah's cage were already on the train. The two natives stood at the temple door, their faces set. They said good-by quickly. Together the tall Lolo chieftain and the little Moso hunter watched the boy they had come to love walk out of their lives into another world where they could never follow. The quest of the snow leopard was at an end.